'I think you're trying to manipulate me,' accused Marnie.

'I can think of a very good reply to that,' he told her with a wide grin.

Trust him to misinterpret her innocent remark. 'I think you're disgusting, James Dalgleish,' she retorted fiercely.

To her surprise, he sobered right down. 'Yes, I know you do,' he returned quietly. 'And what's more, I know you always have. That's something that bothers me—very much.'

Dear Reader,

This month Caroline Anderson begins a trilogy detailing the loves of three women who work with children and babies at the Audley Memorial Hospital. PLAYING THE JOKER opens with Jo, whose traumatic past she must keep from Alex—a deeply emotional read. Margaret Barker takes us to Bali, while James plans to snare Marnie in SURGEON'S STRATEGY by Drusilla Douglas, and Jenna Reid finds her looks deny her the man she wants in Patricia Robertson's HEART IN JEOPARDY.
  Enjoy!

The Editor

Drusilla Douglas is a physiotherapist who has written numerous short stories—mainly for Scottish-based magazines. Now the luxury of working part-time has provided her with the leisure necessary for writing novels.

Recent titles by the same author:

THE WRONG DIAGNOSIS
PROBLEM PAEDIATRICIAN

SURGEON'S STRATEGY

BY
DRUSILLA DOUGLAS

MILLS & BOON LIMITED
ETON HOUSE   18–24 PARADISE ROAD
RICHMOND   SURREY   TW9 1SR

*First published in Great Britain 1992
by Mills & Boon Limited*

© Drusilla Douglas 1992

*Australian copyright 1992
Philippine copyright 1992
This edition 1992*

ISBN 0 263 77949 1

*Set in 10 on 11½ pt Linotron Times
03-9212-55133*

*Typeset in Great Britain by Centracet, Cambridge
Made and printed in Great Britain*

CHAPTER ONE

WHEN the secretary-cum-receptionist popped her head round the office door that Tuesday lunchtime and asked, 'Are you ready to see Fiona now, Marnie?' Marnie Fraser-Firth asked for just two minutes more. Ten would have been better, but the poor child would be miserable enough already.

Marnie was twenty-eight, looked less and was generally considered to be the dishiest of all the physiotherapists at Duntrune Royal Infirmary. She was also Head of Department, so she saw nothing odd in thinking of a girl barely six years her junior as a child, especially as Fiona was very young for her age. That was probably why she was now in the acute emotional mess Marnie shrewdly suspected.

Thank heaven Lynne Selkirk would be back from maternity leave next month. Lynne would be safe from the predations of Mr James Dalgleish, MS, FRCS, M Ch Orth. His victims were getting younger all the time. He'll be raiding the sixth form of the Academy soon, thought Marnie disgustedly, as she came out from behind her desk and arranged two easy-chairs at a confiding angle, sat down in one and called out, 'OK, when you're ready, Belle.'

The girl who came in had obviously been crying. Her blue eyes were red-rimmed and tears had cut channels in her heavy make-up. Marnie stretched out a hand and said, 'Come and sit down, dear, and tell me why you wanted to see me so urgently.'

Fiona collapsed rather than sat, and when she had

5

finished tearing a paper hankie to shreds she burst out, 'I w-want to give in my notice, Marnie.' Then she burst into tears again.

Marnie hadn't expected anything more than a request to change wards. This was clearly the time to open that bottle of sherry she'd been keeping to celebrate Lynne's return to the fold. She poured two small glasses before saying, gently, 'But you've only been with us a few months, Fiona. Leaving so soon wouldn't look very good on your CV, would it?' She was 'gaein' canny', as they said, having been through all this before when James the Lad took up and discarded Polly Meldrum, who had seemed to be such a sensible lass.

'I know, but. . .' Fiona tossed off her sherry and started to splutter.

'You're not enjoying your work,' prompted Marnie.

'No. Yes. . .that is——'

They were getting nowhere, and half the lunch-hour had gone by already. 'You're shaping up to be such a good physio that I'd hate to lose you,' said Marnie truthfully. 'So how about telling me exactly why you've gone off the job, and then we'll try to find a solution.' Such as poisoning, shooting or otherwise disposing of the hospital Lothario.

'It's James—Mr Dalgleish,' Fiona began.

Pretend you haven't heard a thing, Marnie. 'I can't believe he's not pleased with your work, or he'd have told me.' That was certainly true.

'He—he took me to the yacht club regatta.'

I know, I saw you there, sighed Marnie to herself. Only you were too starry-eyed to notice me, you poor wee scrap.

'And then he took me out to dinner.'

And *then* what? wondered Marnie, who thought she

could guess how the bounder worked. Hadn't he tried it on her more than once—presumably when nothing better offered? 'And then. . .?' she prompted gently.

'N-nothing, Marnie.'

'You mean—that's it? Just the one date?' Incredulity overcame Marnie's technique of tactful probing.

'It wasn't just like that.' Fiona swallowed a sob. 'He used to tease me a lot—single me out for notice. Once he gave me a lift home—and another time, he bought me a coffee after work. All the student nurses said he was after me, and I was—was. . .'

'Flattered?'

'And thrilled. He's so marvellous.'

Fiona was perilously near to tears again, and Marnie decided it was time for a small dose of reality. 'Fiona, dear, there's hardly a girl in the whole hospital who doesn't think so—you must know that. And also that Mr Dalgleish has a reputation for—for getting through rather more girlfriends than the average.' How very restrained I'm being! she thought.

'But I thought I was different. He *said* so!' Of course he did! 'And then, after that wonderful Saturday, he just—well, almost ignored me. Several times I tried to get him to tell me what I'd done wrong——' Oh, sweetie, you *are* young for your age! '—but he always managed to—to divert me. And I feel so humiliated. Everybody knew he took me out—and now I can't bear to see him every day. So I want to give in my notice.'

Careful, Marnie. Don't be too hasty now. . . 'How about a change of unit? Outpatients, perhaps, or——'

'No! I want to leave—go home.'

Home was a tiny village in the Highlands. 'But Fiona, what sort of job could you get there?' asked

Marnie gently. 'Community physiotherapy needs somebody experienced——'

'I shall ask my uncle for a job in his hotel.'

That was too much. 'You *can't* waste your training like that!' Marnie exclaimed. 'Look, honey—Duntrune's a friendly city with a lot to offer, if you'll only give it a chance. If you feel you must leave the Royal, then let me see if I can get you transferred to another hospital.'

'I want to go home,' said Fiona flatly.

Marnie ran a hand through her golden curls. 'You're going on leave anyway next week—so take the rest of this one as well, if it'll help. But don't make any rash decisions you might regret.'

'All right, Marnie,' Fiona agreed at last. 'You're so kind and understanding—a boss in a million. I'd like to please you, only——'

'You mustn't do anything just to please me,' Marnie said earnestly. 'Just ask yourself whether this disappointment is really bad enough for you to throw away your career.'

'Put like that. . .' Fiona began.

'I'll sort something out for you,' promised Marnie. 'After all, what are bosses for?'

And it's largely my fault, she thought, as the door closed behind a rather calmer Fiona. I should never have put her on Orthopaedics in the first place.

There were still some minutes to go before the staff dispersed to their various units for the afternoon, so Marnie buzzed the staff-room to ask the senior physio on Ortho to come and see her. 'I've heard,' said Sonia Graham, coming in and flinging herself down in the chair Fiona had vacated. 'So now what do we do? I'd like to murder James the Lad!'

'Join the queue,' invited Marnie. 'And in answer to

your question, we'll do what we always do when we're in a jam. I shall give you what help I can and take the paperwork home with me.'

'I don't see why you should always be the one to get the sticky end,' Sonia objected.

'Have you got a better idea?' sighed Marnie. 'Anyway, the whole damned mess is my fault—I should never have sent the child to your unit in the first place, but as she came to Duntrune to be with her boyfriend I naturally thought she'd be immune. With two posts vacant and holidays looming, it was either her or Jane—and Jane's so impressionable, she thinks *any* man under fifty is celestial. How the hell did I land myself in this job, Sonia?'

'Because you made such a wonderful job of running the department while poor old Cathy was having her nervous breakdown, and it would have been crass ingratitude on the part of the powers that be to give it to anybody else when she had to retire,' Sonia answered promptly.

'Thanks. I certainly prefer your version to the other one!' Some people at Duntrune Royal Infirmary believed that Marnie had only got the job because her father was Professor of Surgery! 'I've sent Fiona home on leave——'

'You old softie!' interrupted her friend affectionately.

'I'm not so sure about that, but, anyway, that's what I've done. I've one or two things that must be attended to first—then I'll see you on the unit by three at the latest. OK?'

'You'll kill yourself,' warned Sonia, getting to her feet. 'All the same, thanks, love. You're a boss in a million.'

'A boss in a million twice in the one day? What more

could a girl crave?' Marnie asked the empty room as the door closed behind Sonia. She rang for Belle, dictated three letters at a pace that played havoc with Belle's shaky shorthand, rang the unit general manager to try to persuade him that filling her vacant posts was' more patient-friendly than taking on extra admin assistants, gave the laundry manager a verbal bouquet for finding a new and better way of washing uniforms, and finally she cancelled her five-thirty hair appointment. The way today was going, she'd be lucky to shake the dust of this place off her feet by six.

Having discarded her white coat, she changed her blouse and skirt for white tunic and navy trousers, bound up her shining blonde curls with a dark ribbon and set off for the orthopaedic unit. On the way, she collected several wolf whistles from short-sighted chauvinists who didn't recognise her in working gear. Who said that life stopped when you reached the dizzy heights of superintendent?

Marnie found Sonia struggling to get a cast-brace fastened on the leg of a young lad who was playing her up. 'If it isn't my old friend Basher Burns,' said Marnie. 'Have you told the other patients how you used to play croquet for the Boys' Brigade?'

Basher turned green. 'You wouldn't, Miss Firth!'

'I might—if you don't behave. Mrs Graham's time is too valuable to be wasted. Unless, of course, you'd rather stay in bed. . .' And how likely was that, after fourteen weeks immobilised on traction for a badly fractured shaft of femur?

'I'll behave—only dinnae tell, for Gawd's sake! An' you've got to let us up. I'm near scunnered wi' lying here.'

'Of course you shall get up, Basher, dear, and, what's more, I'm here to help,' Marnie assured him.

'Big deal,' sighed the patient, but he gave no more trouble.

'So now what would you like me to do?' asked Marnie of Sonia when they'd got Basher back on to his bed after a shaky turn round the ward on crutches.

'Well, most of Fiona's patients are in the women's ward—she found it hard to cope with all the teasing she got from the men. So could you possibly take over in there?'

'Hand over the folder,' said Marnie, flicking through it and noting a nice mixture of ages and conditions. 'I don't think I can go far wrong with this lot.'

As she didn't know any of the patients, it seemed like a good idea to start at the door and work her way round.

Mrs Bain was first. Last night she had fallen on the stairs up to her flat and sustained a fracture of the upper end of the femur, right inside the hip joint. She also had a long history of chronic bronchitis. James the Lad had operated on her early this morning and, although she was round from the anaesthetic, she wasn't quite with it yet. 'I dinnae care for this hotel,' she began. 'They've no' got the right to keep a body in her bed against her will. And another thing—I hope they shot that dog!'

'Which dog?' Marnie was beginning to regret her boast that she couldn't go wrong in here.

'The one that bit me. I've such a gash on ma bum as you'd niver believe. And it's that painful. . .'

'Oh, that dog,' said Marnie. 'You can safely forget about him. As for the gash, that's why you're in bed today, my dear—it'd be too painful to get out. But tomorrow—well, we'll see. Have you been coughing at all?'

'Mind your own business!'

Marnie didn't say that was her business. 'I was only wondering if you needed help,' she persisted, but Mrs Bain wasn't listening. She was beaming past Marnie's shoulder as if she'd just caught a glimpse of Paradise.

Marnie turned to see why and came face to face with James Dalgleish, thirty-five years of age, consultant orthopaedic surgeon and flutterer of susceptible female bosoms. He was still in his theatre garb, which provided an excellent view of his strong, bronzed neck and muscular arms with a fine dusting of dark hairs. When confronted with such potent masculinity, not even respectable old ladies were immune, it seemed.

Add a splendid physique, thick dark curly hair only just tinged with grey, deep-set, laughing brown eyes and charm oozing effortlessly from every pore, and it was no wonder that poor wee Fiona had lost her reason.

He was diverted from his purpose by the sight of Marnie; golden-haired, violet-eyed and softly slim. Also poised and very businesslike. 'What have I done to deserve this honour?' he wondered in the deep, resonant baritone that sent shivers up and down the spines of the unprepared.

'Needs must,' Marnie returned coolly. 'Fiona Watson has—gone missing.' There, now, that ought to shake him!

It didn't. He didn't even frown—just said with a droll shake of the head, 'These youngsters! They take the day off just whenever they feel like it. Not like our generation, eh, Marnie?'

Marnie bristled inwardly. Thank you for nothing, James Dalgleish! she thought. I'm nearer Fiona's age than yours! 'But have you finished with this lady?' he was asking now. 'Because if not I'll come back later.'

Marnie had to admit there were very few consultants

who would offer to do that. 'I couldn't dream of hindering you,' she said graciously. 'Besides, I've lots of other patients to see.' And with that she walked away.

She knew him well enough to know exactly what he'd be doing now. Sitting on the bed with the patient's hand in his, he would chat to her for a minute or two, putting her at ease before the upsetting business of examination. And he'd probably cope better than she had with the tricky problem of the dog bite. He might be a gifted Lothario, but he was an even better surgeon and psychologist. Still, nobody was all bad—or so it was said.

The next patient for treatment was sitting beside her bed, knitting. 'How do you feel about some exercises, Mrs King?' Marnie asked.

'Lovely, dear, but first I'm needing—a wee walk to the toilet,' Mrs King mouthed discreetly.

'I'll come with you, then, and check your walking as we go,' Marnie decided.

When they got back, James was waiting and putting in the time by pouring a drink for another patient. That was something else about him—he was never too proud to render such little services. 'When you've settled Mrs King, I'd like a word with you, please, Miss Fraser-Firth,' he said. He never forgot patients' names either. A perfect paragon, in fact—professionally speaking, that was. Perhaps he needed his interesting private life to balance out such professional perfection!

'Marnie?' His bright eyes were questioning.

'Sorry, I've got a million things on my mind today. You wanted a word. . .'

Marnie was surprised that he only moved to the centre of the ward. They would probably not be overheard there, but she for one was not going to discuss her staff so publicly. 'The office, perhaps?' she hinted.

'There's no point; the X-rays'll not be up here yet. Or do you have a sudden urge to be alone with me?' he suggested with a wicked grin that showed his excellent teeth.

That would be the sort of remark that had so misled poor little Fiona, but not by the faintest flush did Marnie show that she'd even heard. 'My mistake, James. I assumed you wished to talk staff problems, but obviously this is something to do with a patient.'

'You've got it.' He perched carelessly on the corner of the table, arms crossed. 'Mrs Bain could be a problem. It was a simple fracture, but she's wildly osteoporotic, and you know what can happen when one starts tinkering with bone of that sort. So, rather than risk making things worse while screwing the bits together, I gave her an arthroplasty. The best approach was posterior, so I don't want her sitting up yet. And as she's chronically chesty, she'll need careful watching in that department too.'

'I'll bear all that in mind,' Marnie responded calmly. 'Was there anything else?'

James pushed himself upright, assessing her thoughtfully. 'Something happened to you when you got the boss's job,' he said.

'Yes; I grew up. It's a good idea to do that—when you get the boss's job. Unfortunately, not everybody manages it. And now I'd better get back to work, I think.'

That had been a good thrust, but it wouldn't have found its mark. James Dalgleish was too well armoured, both by his own outsize conceit and all the adulation he got.

Back to Mrs King, whose hip movements were better

than usual, so soon after her replacement. 'Shall I cut down on the exercises, then?' she wondered, when congratulated. 'It takes up an awful lot of time, and I'm needing to get this sweater finished for my wee granddaughter's birthday.'

'Very praiseworthy, Mrs King, but it's not just movement we're after here. You've got a lot of muscle-building to do too—they all got rather weak when you seized up and couldn't get about much before your op. So exercises first, and knitting second for the next two weeks, you hear?'

'If you say so—you're the boss.'

'I'll give you a hand with yer knittin', Maisie—if you show us how,' offered the girl in the next bed. 'I'm fair scunnered wi' lying here like this wi' ma ruddy leg screwed to this Eiffel Tower thing!'

A pawky wee teenager with spiky, dyed black hair and eyes like a lemur in the middle of all that make-up. Marnie smiled at her and consulted her list, ident-ifying Jinty McQuaid; pillion passenger on a motor-cycle, with multiple fractures of right tibia and fibula, now being treated in an Oxford brace. 'Why did they no' open up ma leg and pin the bones together, miss?' asked Jinty. 'This is a terrible thing to weigh a body down wi'.'

'I never yet met a patient who likes that, but the fact is it's much the best for fractures like yours. The end result is good, and there's much less scarring, too,' Marnie assured her.

Jinty shrugged. 'I always wear jeans.'

'Suppose you want a holiday in the sun? To Spain, perhaps?'

'On what I get from the YTS? Dinnae be daft, hen!'

'It says here that you're training to be a hairdresser.'

'I was,' corrected Jinty firmly. 'They'll have taken on some other body by now.'

Marnie made a mental note to ask the medical social worker what arrangements were made for cases like this. 'I'd guess there'll be some time in your life when you'll want to show your legs off, Jinty, and then you'll be glad you haven't got a great gash down your shin,' she said.

'Gerroff,' said Jinty, tired of being talked to. 'What brand of colour d'you use on yer hair?'

'I don't,' said Marnie, blinking. 'It's natural.'

'Niver!' Jinty reached out and pulled Marnie down to have her roots checked. 'Jeez, yer right! Are you not the lucky one? How old are you?'

'Older than I look,' returned Marnie firmly. 'And now we'll have less chat and more work, young lady. I want to see that knee bending to a right angle before I leave this ward tonight.'

'Whit's a right angle?' queried Jinty.

'I'll tell you when you get there. Meanwhile, keep trying.'

Judy Geddes was much less chatty. In fact, she was quite withdrawn. But then two broken legs and a back injury three weeks before your degree finals was the darndest luck. Still, if you would go scaling Ben Nevis in the rain. . .

Judy went through her routine with hardly a word. Perhaps Sister had put her next to Jinty, hoping Jinty could draw her out.

Miss Marshall had dislocated her shoulder and had a fracture in it too, which fairly complicated things for somebody living alone. She was waiting to go to the convalescent hospital as soon as they had a free bed. 'I'll be sorry though,' she confided. 'Everybody here is so nice.'

'I promise you you'll love it out at Birchcroft, Miss Marshall,' Marnie told her. 'Acres and acres of lovely parkland to amble round in. . .'

'But they're going to build a new hospital in the grounds.'

'So it's said, but I doubt they'll manage to get it up before you've been and gone, though.'

'Can I have that in writing?' laughed the patient as she showed Marnie how hard she'd been working at her exercises.

Mrs Troy and Mrs Anderson both had fractured necks of femur which had been pinned. They lived side by side in retirement flats. 'We do everything together,' said Mrs Troy, 'so the warden wasn't surprised when Senga here bust her leg two days after I did mine. I'd just got up on the table to clean ma centre light when there was this thundering great knocking on ma door. Well. . .!'

Marnie had helped Mrs Anderson up on to her bed, and they were halfway through her exercise programme by the time Mrs Troy had finished her description of 'My Accident'. Fortunately, they didn't extend their everything-together act to their chatter.

'You've never finished this ward!' exclaimed Sonia when she came to find Marnie saying goodnight to her last patient.

'I hope so—I don't think I've missed anybody out.'

Sonia scanned the list. 'No, everybody's ticked off. Is experience not a wonderful thing?'

'Oh, sure, but, even with my invaluable help, you're still late, Sonia. I just hope I can give you more time tomorrow, though,' said Marnie as the two girls walked back to their own department to change. 'I've some outpatients coming in after lunch. . .'

'But now I hope you're going home,' said Sonia firmly.

'Just one or two wee jobs——'

'That should have got done this afternoon—I know. But I'm so grateful to you.'

'What are bosses for?' asked Marnie as they parted at the door of her office. She sat down at the desk. Sign those letters and then finish making up the week-end and evening duty rosters, because the girls liked plenty of notice so that they could organise their social lives. Oh, dear, still a heap of stuff in the 'IN' tray. Marnie found some brown paper and string and made it into a parcel, intending to sort through it after supper that night.

Ten minutes later she was stowing her homework into the boot of her little car. 'I do hope you're not appropriating NHS property,' observed James Dalgleish, right behind her.

Marnie looked up at him with an expression of mock terror. 'OK, it's a fair cop,' she smiled. 'Those are the departmental records—and I'm going to blackmail all the patients.'

He laughed aloud. 'You can be so nice when you bother,' he said appreciatively. 'What a pity that most of the time you're so stiff and unapproachable.'

'Thanks, James. That's quite the nicest thing you could possibly have said to me,' she returned calmly. 'Heads of Department aren't supposed to be enter-tainers, you know.'

He shrugged. 'As to that, I prefer the old saying about laughter being the best medicine. You're very late tonight, Marnie,' he added.

'And so are you.'

'Yes, but I'm on tonight.'

'While I, alas, am never off—thanks to my eternal staff problems.' To which you contribute! she thought.

Marnie moved round to the offside and got in. James followed, holding on to the door to prevent her driving off. 'Talking of which, I suppose you've told the police?' he queried.

'That I'm setting up as a blackmailer? Not likely!' All the same, she had an inkling what lay behind his question, but she meant to make him spell it out.

'You said this afternoon that young Fiona Watson had gone missing. I took that to mean she was merely playing truant, but if she really is missing then it's a police matter.'

'Would you care?' Marnie asked bluntly.

'What an extraordinary question!' His surprise appeared to be absolutely genuine. 'Of course I'd care. She's a nice wee lassie. A bit immature perhaps, but quite sweet in her way.'

Marnie felt a sudden surge of anger, because that nice, immature, sweet wee lassie was half out of her mind, thanks to him! 'You really are the end, James Dalgleish!' she breathed angrily. 'If I had my way, I'd—I'd lock you up and throw away the key!' If that didn't flatten him, then nothing would.

But the man was impossible; he was actually grinning. 'Thanks, Marnie,' he said. 'That's the nicest thing you could possibly have said, I'd no idea you felt that way about me.'

Marnie could only gasp soundlessly at such effrontery, but she soon got her voice back. 'You are without question the most conceited man it's ever been my misfortune to know!' she informed him, before snatching the door from his grasp and reversing out with much screeching of tyres. If he managed to cap that—and he would—she didn't have to stay and listen.

* * *

The first thing Marnie did on getting home to her smart and luxurious penthouse flat was to take a prepared meal from Marks and Spencer out of the freezer and pop it into the microwave. Then she phoned Dominic Keith, the man in her life. He answered almost at once.

'Dominic?' asked Marnie. 'Would you mind very much if we didn't have that drink tonight? I had to take over for one of my staff today, which has left me with a mountain of paperwork.'

'No problem, dear—I'm fairly snowed under myself. The Kleinson deal, you know.' Dominic was a merchant banker.

'Yes, how is that going?' asked Marnie brightly. She made a point of taking an interest in Dominic's work, as he tried to in hers.

They talked about the deal for a few minutes, and then Dominic said not to forget the new play at the repertory theatre on Friday, to which Marnie replied just try and stop her. She looked at her watch and realised her dinner must be ready. 'Till Friday, then, dear.'

'Lovely, dear.'

Theirs was such a convenient relationship. No strings, no jealousies, and always somebody there for evenings out; the opera, the theatre, concerts, quiet dinners in discreet little restaurants. . . They'd even tried a weekend away once, but that hadn't been exactly earth-moving for either of them, so without analysing it, they'd gone back to the mixture as before.

Just occasionally Marnie felt a vague unrest; a slight dissatisfaction with her life—mostly when she saw bonny, bouncing babies in prams. But it faded when she looked at those of her friends who were juggling family and a career, and paying a price of irritability and chronic fatigue. I'm really so lucky, she told herself, looking round her spacious living-room with its terrace which overlooked the Trune, Scotland's best salmon river. No family worries, a job I love and a salary that most physios don't reach till well into their thirties.

Marnie had never been in love.

CHAPTER TWO

IT WAS no use expecting the staff to be punctual if you didn't set an example, so Marnie was first in next morning as usual. The first thing she noticed was the state of the waiting-room floor, and a lightning tour revealed the whole department to be equally neglected. This was serious when a lot of the patients had open wounds. Marnie went into the office, picked up the phone and dialled the domestic superintendent's number. There was no reply. She tended to forget that not everybody liked to be at their desks by eight-fifteen.

She went to find a mop and bucket, washed the floor of the main treatment-room first and was energetically sluicing out the preparation-room when Sonia arrived, yawning. 'Have you been here all night?' she asked.

Marnie grinned. 'Not quite. I got my usual six and a half hours, but I seem to be standing in for the cleaner today. And as Belle's away to the dentist, I'm afraid it'll be at least ten before I can get up to help you.'

'Sounds all right to me,' said Sonia. 'Not even a wonder woman like you can be in two places at once.'

Having washed the most important floors, Marnie tried the domestic super again, and this time she got an answer. 'Ai'm very short of staff,' announced that lady in what was known locally as a pan-loaf accent.

'I am too, Mrs Wood, so I can sympathise, but——'

'And Ai have the unit manager's permission to use mai discretion. So Ai'm leaving all non-essential areas today.'

If anything was calculated to get Marnie's dander up, it was being classed as non-essential. A chance glance across the road at the office block enabled her to say firmly, 'I can see cleaners at work in Admin, Mrs Wood, and, if they deal with as many open wounds over there as my staff do here, then I'll be very surprised indeed. I've given the place a perfunctory mop-over myself, but I must insist that some attempt is made to clean the treatment-rooms properly before our surgical patients are brought down.'

'That is quait out of the question, Miss Firth. Ai am very short of staff.'

'Then may I suggest you do as I do in such circumstances, which is almost all of the time? I roll up my sleeves and muck in with the workers!' Marnie put down the phone, frowning. She wasn't proud of that outburst, but the woman was impossible, and Marnie wasn't about to let her get away with it. She pulled the memo pad towards her and wrote: 'To Unit General Manager from Superintendent Physiotherapist. While fully aware of the shortage of domestic staff, I would stress the necessity for absolute cleanliness in my department, where open wounds, blah, blah, blah. . .' Copies to Senior Nursing Officer, all consultants and Domestic Superintendent. They would have to take notice. There were pluses as well as drawbacks in being the Professor of Surgery's only daughter—they couldn't risk her carrying tales to Daddy!

Now she'd better open the mail, just in case there was something urgent. Oh, goody! Here was somebody wanting a job. Take the main details for reference and pop the application into an envelope for Personnel. Now what next? An electronics firm wanting to sell some new piece of equipment. Sounds marvellous, but Finance will only tell me we can't afford it. Now

supposing I can persuade Meditronics to let us have it
on loan, for clinical trials, then I can get consultant
backing if it turns out to be better than anything else
we've got. And then they'll *have* to buy it for me. . .
Nothing much else, so now for a quick change into
uniform and escape to the wards before anything else
crops up.

Marnie didn't manage it, of course. The phone rang
non-stop for the next half-hour, and Mr James
Dalgleish's weekly ward-round had begun in the
women's ward by the time she made it to Ortho. So
poor old Sonia was going to be even more pushed for
time today. Take the maintenance class in the men's
ward for her, then, Marnie. She's never much liked
that.

'Look out, lads, it's the head torturer,' said Basher
Burns when Marnie walked in.

'With eyes like that, she can torture my head—and
anything else she fancies,' riposted a freckle-faced lad
with streetwise eyes who was languishing on traction
like almost half the ward. The city of Duntrune was
near a motorway, and the orthopaedic surgeons were
constantly bewailing the high proportion of emergencies that held up their elective procedures, such as joint
replacements.

Marnie peered at Freckle-face's unimpressive leg
muscles. 'You could do with some strong electrical
current for those, m'lad,' she remarked, then having
temporarily silenced him, she turned to Basher. 'Played
much croquet lately?' she enquired on a murmur, while
threatening vengeance with a look. With their leaders
unexpectedly vanquished, the rest of the lads soon
quietened down.

The maintenance exercises devised to maintain
muscle tone and joint range of movement in all joints

not actually immobilised were not all suitable for every patient, so Marnie dashed round the ward making a lightning assessment of who could do what and who mustn't. Then she took the class, interspersing instructions with humorous comments to lift the monotony. By the end, she had them practically eating out of her hand. In fact, they were so well behaved that Marnie began to wonder. Turning round, she saw the ward-round retinue poised in the doorway. 'I was just beginning to realise that all this peace and quiet wasn't down to my magnetic personality,' she admitted with a smile. 'I must apologise for holding you up, Mr Dalgleish.'

'Not at all, Miss Fraser-Firth. We've only just arrived, and watching you all at work was most instructive.' Oh, yes, James the Lad knew how to behave when he must. Never do anything to undermine the credibility of a colleague in front of patients. 'Are we to have the pleasure of your company on this round?' he asked.

'No, sir. I'm acting junior at the moment, so I'll be taking myself off to the women's ward now.'

'In that case. . .' James took her by the elbow and ushered her outside.

Smiling, she freed herself. 'But there's no need to treat me like a junior,' she reproved him.

'If only you'd cut off those beautiful curls and hide your remarkable eyes behind dark glasses, then I might just manage to remember how important you are,' he returned easily. 'But to business. There's a new admission asking for you most particularly. Apparently you treated her as an outpatient recently. She's a Mrs Gray, and she has a very nasty tib and fib which I must do something about as soon as she's digested her breakfast. Be sure to have a word with her, will you?

She's as nervous as a kitten and needs all the reassurance she can get.'

'Of course I will. I remember her well. She came to me for cervical spondylosis.'

'Ever the model physio,' he commented. 'Do your girls find it very hard to live up to you?'

'If you want a truthful answer, then you'd better ask them,' suggested Marnie, putting a thumb on the bleeper in her top pocket, to silence its sudden buzzing. But by then James was already back in the ward.

Marnie went into Sister's office and dialled the switchboard, to find it was the chief personnel officer calling to tell her that he'd finally got around to advertising her staff vacancies. She refrained from asking how much money they'd saved on salaries, while her overworked girls strove to maintain cover, and asked instead about the possibility of arranging a transfer to the Western General Hospital for Fiona. 'Miss Craig would be willing to have her,' Marnie added. And why not, when every department in the city was short of staff?

When he asked why Fiona wanted to leave so soon, Marnie lied in her teeth, saying that she lived near there—true—and it was costing her too much to travel—false.

'Hey, you!' called Jinty the second Marnie entered the ward. She had no idea that Marnie was the head physio and wouldn't have cared if she had. 'I'm wantin' a bit of your hair for testin'.'

'You don't believe it's not dyed,' guessed Marnie, amused.

'I do, but ma boss doesnae. He was in last night, visitin' us. So he asked me to get him a bit—for interest.'

If her boss had been visiting, then that was a hopeful

sign. Could be he was keeping her place open for her, after all. 'Always willing to oblige,' said Marnie, 'but I'm not going to take a cutting and upset the line. You'll need to wait until I go for a trim. Will that do?'

'I guess so,' returned Jinty, while Judy said that anybody'd think Miss Firth was a plant, the way they were talking.

Thus encouraged by her apparent lightening of mood, Marnie treated Judy first today, with Jinty looking on and questioning everything she did. The girl was very intelligent—no doubt about it.

Mrs Bain was quite lucid today and ready to take Marnie to task. 'You said I could get up the day—and look at me lying here!' she began reproachfully.

'I'm afraid I made a mistake there, Mrs Bain. When I said that, I didn't know that Mr Dalgleish had done a very special kind of operation on your hip, which means you need to lie flat for the first few days.'

'Special, eh? Well, he needn't hae bothered. The bargain offer would've done. Who wants to lie here staring up at yon damp patch on the ceiling?'

'But you can get up to take a few steps from time to time,' Marnie told her. 'As long as you don't bend that hip.'

'I'd like tae see you gettin' in and oot your bed without bending your hips!'

'It's quite possible—with help. I'll show you now if you like.'

That was accomplished with much complaining. 'Ay niver haird the like,' sniffed the patient. 'Sich nonsense! I'll be checking up on you.'

'If you like, Mrs Bain, but I got my instructions from Mr Dalgleish himself,' Marnie assured her.

Marnie was sitting on the bed and holding the hand of her old friend Mrs Gray when James came to tell

her she'd soon be going to Theatre. You had to admire
the way he always had time for the personal touch.
Some surgeons at his level hardly ever saw a conscious
patient!

When Marnie got up to leave, James thanked her
with a smile she had some difficulty in ignoring. Poor
wee Fiona, she thought. How could she possibly have
stood up to him? If I'd had somebody like him chasing
after me at her age, I might well have come a cropper
too.

'Marnie, could we give Basher a quick whizz round
the ward before lunch?' asked Sonia, breaking in on
those weighty thoughts.

'Surely. Lead on, love. You're the boss up here.'

Lunch for Marnie was cheese and an apple in her
office, while she sorted out the morning's hiccups with
Belle. Belle wasn't eating anything after her session
with her dentist. 'Are you well enough to be here at
all?' wondered Marnie when she saw Belle's face, all
swollen and red.

'Better this than the ironing,' said Belle firmly. 'What
shall I do about this request from the Academy for
somebody to speak to fifth-formers at a careers seminar
on Saturday week?'

'Tell them, yes—and I'll do it if there are no
volunteers.'

'Surprise, surprise,' said Belle, writing that down.
'But don't forget the hospital fête.'

'Don't worry, it's more than my life's worth to miss
that! It doesn't start until two, so I should make it
easily if I go straight there from the Academy.'

Her few outpatients treated successfully, Marnie
managed to get back to Ortho by half-past two, which
she thought was quite good.

Sonia thought it was miraculous. 'Especially as you

get through twice as much as Fiona did in the same
time,' she added.

Marnie said that was one of the advantages of getting
old, before dashing off to complete her day's work.

She found Jinty scratching her damaged leg with one
of Mrs King's knitting needles. 'Don't do that,' she
scolded. 'You could get an infection.'

'But it's that damn itchy—you've no idea!' protested
Jinty.

'Then I'll fetch some olive oil.'

'I'm no' a ruddy lettuce,' yelled Jinty as Marnie sped
away.

'I'm no' wantin' that pongy stuff on me,' she complained when Marnie returned.

'It doesn't pong, and it's the best thing I know for
clearing away dry skin,' said Marnie, dabbing energetically at Jinty's leg. 'See how it's fetching it off? We
always advise this for legs newly out of plaster. And
don't tell me you've not been in plaster, because it
comes to the same thing, when you can't wash.'

'Jeez, but you're the sharp one! You want to mind
you don't cut yourself,' advised Jinty. 'Are ye wantin'
me to do ma knee exercises again?'

'Of course. You're still not bending enough.'

'Fiona only made us do 'em once a day.'

'I'm not Fiona,' said Marnie firmly.

'You can say that again! She's no' a natural blonde,
for a start.'

Mrs King was all puffed up with pride. 'I got full
marks from Mr Dalgleish on the round. He says he's
never known one of his hip replacements do better
than me.' In Marnie's experience, all James's hips did
very well indeed, but this was just another example of
his deft touch with patients. 'I'm not to get home any
sooner, though,' Mrs King lamented.

'That's because Mr Dalgleish wants to make sure the new joint is firmly in place before you're allowed to roam free, Mrs King.'

'Almost his exact words, dear, so I know you're right.'

Who can hope to hold a candle to such a divinity? thought Marnie, as she suggested trying a full flight of stairs today.

Mrs Troy and Mrs Anderson were next in the rehab stakes, and then it was time to talk to James's new admissions about their pre-and post-op routines. By then Mrs Gray was back from Theatre and still a bit woozy. She was also inclined to be sick. Marnie was holding the bowl for her and wiping her mouth when James came in to check up on her.

He nodded approvingly. 'I'm glad to see you've kept the common touch, despite your elevated position,' he said in a low voice to Marnie, before smiling at the patient. He put a cool hand on her perspiring forehead. 'Sorry about this, my dear, but it can happen to any of us. I was as sick as a dog when I had surgery after getting knocked out by a boom while sailing.'

'You weren't, Mr Dalgleish!'

'I was—and very glad of it. I've been much more sympathetic towards my patients ever since.'

'I can't believe you were ever anything but sympathetic,' Mrs Gray insisted.

Marnie left them to admire each other and went to see if Sonia was wanting to get Basher up for another circuit. Lads of his age usually got the hang of hopping along with crutches much sooner than this, and the two physios were still discussing his poor performance when they left the ward half an hour later.

As they passed the open door of the office, James called out to Marnie. She sighed. 'Now what?' she wondered aloud. 'Ah well, you go on, Sonia, I can deal with him.'

'I don't doubt that,' laughed her friend. 'OK, then— see you tomorrow.'

Marnie went no further than the office doorway. 'Yes, James?' she said.

'Why is it she always manages to make me feel like a naughty houseman?' he asked, staring into space with a comically soulful expression.

Marnie managed not to say that was probably because that was how he often behaved—even superintendent physiotherapists mustn't be quite so outspoken to consultants. She took two small steps nearer. 'You wished to speak to me,' she reminded him with the utmost courtesy, entirely unmoved by his provocative look.

He shrugged resignedly, accepting that he wasn't going to get a rise out of her. Then he said matter-of-factly, 'I have a favour to ask of you, Marnie—a professional favour,' he stressed. 'I'm sure you know that for years past your opposite number at the Western General has given talks on physiotherapy to medical students just starting on their clinical work?' Marnie nodded. 'Unfortunately, she's gone down with some bug or other just as they're due to begin, and I was wondering if you could possibly deputise for her.' He looked at her beseechingly.

I expect he thinks I'll never be able to refuse when he looks at me like that, thought Marnie. 'My calendar's full to bursting,' she began, 'but Emily Craig has been very kind to me over the years, so I'll do it, if only to relieve her mind. How much time do I have to prepare?'

'Would you like to sit down before I tell you?' James asked scaringly.

'I suppose that means next week,' sighed Marnie.

'Worse than that, my dear. The first group is scheduled for tomorrow afternoon.'

Marnie ran a distracted hand through her luxuriant curls, leaving them looking very untidy. 'Oh, heavens—that means I've only got tonight!'

'And you've got a date,' supposed James, viewing this vulnerable Marnie with lively interest.

'No, I've not, fortunately.' She frowned. 'Did you really not know about this before, James?'

'Cross my heart,' he breathed—impressive stuff, but meaningless when you remembered that he hadn't got one. 'I'll tell you what I'll do, though. I'll have them come here instead of to the General, and then at least you'll be in your own department with your own equipment with which to demonstrate.'

'Thanks for that, anyway. What time?'

'Half three—or later, if that suits you better. Most of 'em will be here anyway for practical teaching, so it should work out all right.'

'Oh, sure—but for whom?' Marnie wondered with a sigh.

'It's years since I've seen you at a loss like this, Marnie,' said James Dalgleish, sounding as though he found that cause for regret.

'That could all be about to change,' she told him with another big sigh. 'Still, I guess it can't be helped, when Emily is ill.' She knew better than to ask if the students' tightly packed schedule could be changed.

'There'll be a cheque coming your way from the university, of course,' he told her.

'Then I hope it's big enough to buy the wherewithal to drown my sorrows afterwards,' said Marnie, trying to look on the bright side.

'As to that, special catering arrangements are always

made for guest lecturers,' he returned with a bright, speculative glance.

'Dinner at the Queen's would hardly be sufficient in this case,' she insisted, 'but I'd better hurry off home and get started on my spiel. I can see it's going to be a long night.'

'But a blameless one,' said James with a wicked chuckle which Marnie pretended not to hear.

She sat up very late working on her talk, covering sheets and sheets of paper in the process. By one a.m. she had condensed these to a dozen. She wondered why she had gone to so much trouble when all she was required to do was to give a bunch of students their first introduction to physiotherapy. It wasn't that simple, though. Those students would one day be doctors, and their career-long attitude to her profession could be coloured by the impression she made on them tomorrow.

Marnie didn't sleep well and worried all the way to work next morning. Belle was the first to notice her abstraction. 'You're in love,' she said, going for the most interesting possibility.

'Don't be daft, Belle,' Marnie returned automatically. 'Anyway, who is there for me to be in love with?'

'How about Dominic? You've certainly been going out with him for long enough. Probably too long,' added Belle. 'Have you ever wondered if it might be time for a change?'

'Right now, the only change I'm planning to make is in the big gym—somewhere around three o'clock this afternoon.' Marnie told Belle about the lecture-demonstration that had been sprung on her the day before, and how she planned to cope. Then she gave Belle a list of the chores she wanted attended to

beforehand. 'And don't let the head porter fob you off
with fairy-tales when you ask for help to move the
heavy equipment,' she advised. 'Tell him this is for Mr
Dalgleish's students on Mr Dalgleish's orders. He
thinks the world of him since James the Lad operated
so successfully on his daughter's deformed foot.'

'Now there's a man who *is* a man,' considered Belle,
and she didn't mean the head porter, as Marnie knew
just fine.

At least everybody's hero will not be getting in my
hair today, she reflected when she was at last able to
join Sonia on Ortho. Thursday was James's planned
ops day, and he'd made a very early start. By the time
Marnie had parked her car that morning, the lights
were already blazing in Theatre.

Sonia met her with the news that Basher was to be
seen by a neurologist. 'We're not the only ones who've
been worrying about his balance,' she said. 'James the
Lad was sufficiently disturbed by his rotten performance on the round to give him a thorough going-over
last night.'

'Does that man never take any time off?' wondered
Marnie. It had been nearly seven when she herself left
the ward last night.

'Don't be silly, dear,' said Sonia. 'However do you
suppose he got his reputation if he doesn't?'

'Good point. Shall we get Basher up now, then,
before I start on the girls?'

All morning, Marnie kept having ideas about her
afternoon talk, and the fourth time Jinty saw her take
out her notebook, she asked, 'Are you writin' a piece
for the papers, or what?'

Marnie explained about the student session, to which
Jinty responded, eyes sparkling, that if Marnie needed

a patient for a model she'd be glad to help out. 'I could do with a bit of handlin' from an expert,' she said.

'I doubt your average student is an expert,' returned Marnie, taking out her goniometer to measure Jinty's knee and see if it was anywhere near the goal she'd set for it.

Jinty gave a filthy snigger. 'Depends what you're lookin' for, hen,' she said. 'We all ken aboot medical students.'

Despite going non-stop all morning, Marnie knew she wasn't going to get everybody treated. 'And I'll not manage to get back this afternoon either, Sonia,' she apologised as they returned to base at lunchtime. 'By the time I've treated my outpatients, it'll be time to get ready for the invasion.'

'And how do you feel about that?' asked Sonia.

'The invasion? Terrified!'

'You'll knock 'em cold,' Sonia prophesied confidently.

Marnie remembered that when the students started trickling into the big gym. The only cold things in this room are my feet, she thought wryly.

But once started on her talk, she soon gained confidence. As always in a group of that sort, there was one smart-alec out to trip her up, but his attempts were soon submerged in a barrage of genuine interest from the others. The session lasted more than twice as long as Marnie had expected, and she was wondering how she could bring it to a close when the door opened to admit James Dalgleish. He stood a moment, surveying the scene. Some students were trying out the weight and pulley systems, while others were trying out the different electrical currents. Then he strolled over to the group to whom Marnie was demonstrating a particular massage technique that dramatically improved the circulation.

'It looks to me as though you're trying to pack three years' training into one afternoon, Miss Fraser-Firth,' he observed humorously.

Marnie looked up at him, bright-faced and animated. 'It's been a great pleasure talking to them, Mr Dalgleish. They're all so interested.'

'I wish I could command the same degree of attention,' said James, looking fixedly at a student who had cut his last lecture. It was said of James Dalgleish that he never forgot a face. 'However, as it's now almost six-thirty——' Marnie gasped unbelievingly '—I'd say you've all had your money's worth. So off home with you—and make a note of all you've seen and heard today. I'm thinking of asking Miss Fraser-Firth to set you a paper later on.'

There were groans all round, and then one of the students thanked Marnie very nicely on behalf of them all. When they had gone, James took another look at all the equipment, books and pamphlets Marnie had on show. 'You've really gone to town,' he observed appreciatively. 'But then you never do anything by halves, do you, Marnie?'

'Not if I can help it. Besides, I'm being paid for this, am I not?'

'Which reminds me—the first payment is due as soon as you can get out of that uniform.' Marnie stared at him, frowning. 'And into your street clothes,' he added, watching her discomfiture with undisguised enjoyment.

'What in the world are you talking about?' she demanded crossly.

'I always take Emily Craig out for a meal,' he explained. 'So I can hardly do less for you.'

'Oh, I think you can,' said Marnie, once she'd got her breath back. 'Emily does six of these sessions, and I've only done one.'

'So far,' he said. 'But we don't yet know how long Emily is going to be out of action.'

'I think you're trying to manipulate me,' accused Marnie.

'I can think of a very good reply to that,' he told her with a wide grin.

Trust him to misinterpret her innocent remark! 'I think you're disgusting, James Dalgleish!' Marnie retorted fiercely.

To her surprise, he sobered right down. 'Yes, I know you do,' he returned quietly. 'And what's more, I know you always have. That's something that bothers me—very much. But to return to the present—it's quite true that I take Emily out for dinner as a thank-you. You can ask her if you don't believe me.'

Marnie was finding this unknown, quiet and earnest James surprisingly difficult to deal with. 'You wouldn't tell me to check with her if that wasn't true,' she returned evenly, 'but it so happens I have a date tonight.'

'I don't believe you,' he answered, just as evenly. 'If you had, you'd have sent the students packing long since.'

Oh, but he was shrewd. 'It's—a late date.'

James shrugged. 'Have it your way, Marnie—I'm not going to beg. But thank you very much for helping out so splendidly today. You did a grand job.'

He swung round and walked out then, leaving Marnie feeling vaguely disappointed. Why? Had she thought they would go on sparring until she gave in and agreed to go for dinner with him? And supposing she had? Where would have been the harm? Good grief, he'd only been suggesting a meal—not a *grande affaire*! And heaven knew she was hungry enough. And it would have been nice not to have to prepare something after such a long and tiring day.

Well, Marnie could still avoid that, even though now she'd have to pay for herself. As soon as she'd changed out of uniform, she strolled out of the hospital gate and round the corner to a pub called the Waterman, that was usually well patronised by staff from the Royal. Tonight, though, there was nobody in whom she knew, so Marnie dined alone on chicken salad and cheesecake.

Never mind; it was giving her the chance to think over that old saying about cutting off your nose to spite your face.

CHAPTER THREE

BY THE time she walked into her office the following
Monday morning, Marnie had quite forgotten being so
silly as to regret turning down James Dalgleish's invitation to dinner the previous Thursday. Perhaps not
having spoken to him for three days had helped.

When he passed her in the corridor on Friday, with
only the briefest of good afternoons, she was surprised,
not to say piqued. Surely it wouldn't have killed him to
give her the time of day after her heroic efforts on
behalf of the students? Then on reflection, Marnie
realised that was all of a piece with his character—as
she read it. She had deputised nobly for Emily Craig
when he'd asked her to, but had refused his so-called
thank-you afterwards, and James Dalgleish was not
accustomed to snubs. She had succeeded in denting his
outsize conceit, and how many women could say that?

'You're looking very smug,' Sonia had commented
soon after.

Marnie had replied that, in her opinion, she had
every reason to, and Sonia had agreed, going on to say
that not everybody would have coped so well with a
pack of med students at such short notice.

Sonia hadn't got the point, but let it pass. Explaining
might have led her into supposing that Marnie was
more interested in James the Lad than she was—and
that would never do.

Friday evening had been very pleasant; enjoying the
play in Dominic's company and discussing it afterwards
with him, over supper in the little Italian restaurant

opposite the theatre. Dominic was so restrained, so urbane.

On Saturday, he had had to play golf at Gleneagles with clients of his firm, so Marnie had taken the chance to catch up on her washing, shopping and getting her hair done. Then, yesterday, they had driven out to the country to lunch at a small hotel which was said to be building itself a good reputation. The meal had been a disappointment, and Dominic had gone on for rather long about that, but, as it was he who had chosen the place, Marnie let him run on. She paid her share with a smile—they usually went Dutch—and then suggested visiting a nearby stately home, newly opened to the public. As Dominic adored such visits and the chance they gave him to criticise the taste of his so-called betters, he was soon restored to his usual smooth self. They had spent the evening at Marnie's flat, eating scrambled eggs and peaches while listening to Mozart.

All very relaxed and undemanding. But then wasn't that just how Marnie needed her leisure hours to be, when her professional life was so hectic? So here she was on Monday morning, ready for anything the week could bring. Or so she believed.

She started as usual with the mail. Today there were several memos from Admin about such vital things as litter in the car park, using the correct sizes of envelopes and cutting down on overtime. Marnie stared in bewilderment at that one. What did they want her to do? Tell the serious chest cases that they could only cough between the hours of nine and five?

It was a relief to open the next letter and read the heartfelt praise of a grateful patient who had just completed a course of treatment. Marnie laid that aside for Belle to pin on the staff-room noticeboard, before opening the last letter. This proved to be a warmly worded note from James for 'such a brilliant and comprehensive lecture to the medical students, prepared and delivered so willingly and at such short notice'.

Forgetting how she'd resented his brief greeting on Friday, Marnie swung right round to thinking how nice this was of him, when he had already thanked her in person and had so many calls on his time. But then James Dalgleish always did the right thing—professionally, anyway. She must remember to thank him the next time their paths crossed.

Having managed to persuade all her outpatients to come in the afternoons while the staff crisis endured, Marnie was able to get to Orthopaedics quite early that morning. Sonia had already put Basher's cast brace on his damaged leg, so they began by giving him his first walk of the day. He didn't manage his crutches any better than before, and when they were safely out of earshot Marnie asked if the neurologist had been to examine him yet.

'He came on Saturday morning,' returned Sonia, who had been on duty over the weekend. 'He didn't say much, but he wants to see Basher in his clinic in two months' time.'

So he suspects something too, realised Marnie sadly. Basher—accident-prone if ever anybody was—had been known to Marnie since her student days, and, despite his tendency to play her up, she was fond of the lad.

'Perhaps Dr MacNab is just playing safe,' hoped Sonia, who also had a soft spot for him.

'Let's hope so. After all, Basher has always been clumsy, which is why he keeps getting into trouble,' observed Marnie as they went their separate ways.

Things in the women's ward were much the same

with the old stagers, but there had been two new admissions over the weekend. Curiously enough, both had fractured kneecaps. Mrs Stirling had fallen down in the rush to be first into Muir and Donaldson's—Duntrune's answer to Harrods—when the summer sale began on Saturday, while young Louise Fairbairn had been knocked off her bike by a bus. Marnie had just finished assuring them that they would both soon be as good as new when James came into the ward with Sister in fluttering attendance. Mrs Bain had been complaining of pain in the calf of her bad leg, and James suspected a blood clot, judging by his frown as he disappeared behind the drawn curtains.

He looked happier coming out, though, so presumably she was suffering from nothing more serious than cramp. He stopped by Louise's bed to say as much to Marnie. 'So you can continue with routine therapy, Miss Fraser-Firth,' he concluded formally.

'Thank you. And, Mr Dalgleish,' she added hurriedly before he could walk away, 'I'd like to thank you for your note about the medical students. It was kind of you to take the time to write.'

'On the contrary,' he insisted quietly. 'It was kind of you to help me out.' Then he turned to Louise and asked, 'So how's the leg today, young lady?'

'Oh, it's ever so much better, thank you,' she told him, blushing and giggling. 'At least, it was till the physio made me try tightening the muscles——' She stopped, biting her lip. 'Sorry, miss, I wasn't trying to get you into trouble. . .'

'Not to worry,' said James. 'Miss Fraser-Firth would only be in trouble if she hadn't made you exercise, so keep up the good work, both of you.'

He did go then, leaving Marnie feeling oddly dissatisfied with the encounter, though she couldn't for the life of her think why. She soon forgot about him, though, when she started work again. She enjoyed treating orthopaedic cases, and, but for James Dalgleish, always in and out. . .but she'd decided not to think about him, hadn't she? And he certainly didn't cause her any annoyance for the next day or two, because Marnie hardly ever saw him.

On Wednesday afternoon, Marnie happened to glance at the evening duty roster and was reminded that she'd volunteered to work tonight in place of Fiona, who was still on holiday. Now here was a problem. She had arranged to go with Dominic to a private viewing at the Cawdor Art Gallery tonight, and if there was anything Dominic hated, it was having his arrangements upset at the last moment.

Marnie had to ring his office several times before he was free to speak to her. She was tactfully abject, while still managing to make it sound as if DRI would grind to a halt without her presence that night.

As she'd feared, Dominic was most put out. He made a great business of telling her he would be taking his secretary instead, and didn't let her off the phone until she had promised twice not to renege on their date for the Scottish Opera on Friday.

At that point, Belle came flying into the office to say that that young sixth-former from the Academy—the one with the elbow—was having some sort of fit in the main treatment-room and Mrs Abercrombie had gone into hysterics out of sympathy.

By the time Marnie arrived on the scene, both patients had recovered and were starting on the cups of tea which one of the physios had thoughtfully made for them. First, Marnie took the boy aside for a pep talk about keeping up his medication as well as making

sure he had an early appointment for Neurology. Then
she put Mrs Abercrombie through her paces. As well
as being very susceptible to the ills of others, she had a
severely arthritic knee, for which she was awaiting
replacement surgery.

When the physios began to trickle back from the
wards at the end of the day, Marnie set about compiling
her evening list. She viewed it with amazement. As few
as four must be a record, even in summer. She would
do paperwork until seven, have supper in the canteen,
treat the patients and maybe get away as early as half-
eight.

It didn't work out like that. She finished in good
time all right, but when she went to get her car she
found it was completely blocked in by a large transit
van. What that was doing in the staff car park was a
mystery, but there it was, and, until it was shifted,
Marnie couldn't get at her car.

She tried the porters' room, but nobody there knew
anything about it, suggesting that it had probably been
left there for safety, by somebody unconnected with
the hospital. Very likely, when there was so much
vandalism in the neighbourhood, but knowing why
didn't solve Marnie's problem. She bowed to the
inevitable and walked to the bus stop. Her personal
bleep had a radius of five miles, so she'd be in touch all
the way home. If it goes off when I'm on the bus,
though, I'll probably be arrested for a terrorist, she
was thinking, when James Dalgleish's black Audi
purred to a halt alongside the queue.

It always surprised Marnie that he didn't drive
something red and lethal which would have been much
more in keeping with his personality. There were two
young nurses in the queue, and as she didn't want to

witness yet more conquests, Marnie sidled behind a large man and pretended she hadn't noticed the car.

'I thought it was you,' said James, winkling Marnie out of her hiding place. 'Is there something the matter with your car?'

'No, it's just blocked in by a van,' she returned matter-of-factly. 'But it doesn't matter. I'm only going one stop, and by the time I've run my errand I'll probably be able to get it out.'

James raised a derisory eyebrow. 'I hate to think what kind of an errand you've got at the next bus stop,' he said. 'It's right outside that pub where the local tarts go to pick up sailors. You haven't come down to that, have you?'

Even poised and beautiful career girls dressed by Country Casuals had trouble fielding remarks like that. 'I—I'm going to call on an old patient,' Marnie improvised, blushing and wishing she hadn't thought up that stupid explanation.

'He or she must be living rough, then. There's nothing left standing on that corner but the pub.'

'I. . .meant two stops.' Idiot! Why did you not say he's the publican?

'Of course—an easy mistake to make. And in case you haven't noticed, there's the bus going now.'

'Why don't you drop dead?' asked Marnie, with a lack of finesse she'd not descended to since her first and only date with a very randy medical student.

'Because I'm not ready to go yet. Do you want a lift or not? The next bus'll not be along for at least twenty minutes.'

'No, thank you, I prefer to fend for myself,' said Marnie. 'Anyway, I've changed my mind—about visiting.'

'That's the first sensible thing you've said tonight. So

long, then.' And with that, James got back in his car and drove off.

Marnie began to walk back to the hospital, but found her way barred by two skinheads. They must have been watching her exchange with James, because one asked, 'Too expensive for 'im, are ye, darlin'?'

Not for the first time that night, Marnie deplored the run-down dockside neighbourhood in which the Royal Infirmary was located. She took a deep breath and said with great presence of mind, 'Watch what you say. I'm a policewoman on a stake-out.'

'Show us yer warrant card, then,' they said, coming after her and grabbing her arm. For yobs, they were too well clued-up by half.

It was no more than twenty yards to the gate. Should she run for it? Marnie was wondering, when her bleeper went off, fitting in very well with her claim to CID status. Her assailants backed off long enough for Marnie to sprint to safety. From the gate lodge, she phoned the switchboard to find out who was calling her. 'There's been nobody asking for you, Miss Firth, so there must be a fault somewhere,' was the reply.

And the luckiest in my career, she thought, remembering to say 'thank you', before stumbling outside. Her knees were trembling with reaction. In a minute, she would go and see if that van had moved, but first she needed to get herself together.

As it had just a short time before, a sleek black Audi slid to a halt beside her, its passenger door invitingly open. James must have seen those skinheads in his rear-view mirror and driven back. 'I represent the NHS staff rescue service,' he said. 'Now get in, you silly superintendent physiotherapist, before I lose my patience.'

Marnie was still smarting from the memory of her feeble excuses. 'My own car——' she began.

'Is still blocked in. I checked while you were in the lodge.' He leaned across and looked up at her, and his glance was anything but flattering. 'You've got ten seconds—and this time I really will drive off and leave you!'

He was revving the engine all the time it took for Marnie to decide this was no time for standing on her dignity. 'You're very k-i-i-i-nd,' she ended on a half-shriek as the car shot away before she was properly in her seat.

'Belt up,' said James without looking at her.

Marnie did as she was told in both senses. Then she put her briefcase on the floor and held her handbag primly on her knees like a shield. If James spoke to her, she would answer, but not unless.

He didn't need to, because he knew where she lived, and presently they fetched up in fine style in the forecourt. 'That'll be three pounds twenty, please, ma'am,' said James, poker-faced.

Marnie wrestled with an absurd desire to giggle. 'And cheap at the price,' she managed with scarcely a tremor as she opened her bag.

'On the other hand——' he said slowly, just as she produced her purse.

'You'd better have a good alternative, Mr Cabman.'

'If you've got such a thing as a copy of Cairncross on *Inherited Disorders of Calcium Metabolism* in the house, I'd rather have a loan of that. I didn't have time to get to the library today.'

'Sorry,' she said. 'I've never heard of it, and, in any case, it would be a bit too weighty for me. Why not try Andrew Wilkie? He lives in this block too, you know.'

'What? And let him know I don't carry every word
in my head? No, thanks!'

'How vain you are,' considered Marnie.

'I prefer to talk of proper professional pride,' he
retorted loftily, 'but I'm too hungry to debate the
point.' He paused, drumming his fingers lightly on the
steering wheel. 'I suppose you'd have the vapours if I
suggested going for a curry at the Delhi Palace, just
around the corner?'

'That's an—interesting suggestion,' said Marnie, 'but
as I had plaice and chips at the hospital not two hours
ago, I think it would be very unwise to act on it.' She
opened the car door and stepped out. 'Thank you very
much for rescuing me—I'm really grateful. And I hope
you enjoy your curry.'

It was with very real relief that Marnie shut the door
of her flat. That had been some evening, to say the
least. The neat pile of mail on the hall table told that
the agency cleaners had been. Eagerly she went
through it, hoping for a letter from her father, who was
now some ten days into his US lecture tour. She sighed.
Nothing but a bill and the usual helping of junk mail.

Glancing up, she caught sight of herself in the mirror,
and gasped aloud. Her hair had come down in a riotous
Moll Flanders sort of way, her cheeks were flushed,
her eyes brilliant, and her blouse was unbuttoned,
practically down to the waist. Marnie was appalled.
One of those louts had certainly grabbed her arm and
she'd had to sprint. But this? What must the gate
porter have thought? And James? As she thought of
him, her full pink mouth compressed into a thin, hard
line. If proof were needed that he was no gentleman,
this was it. A decent man would have found some way
to let her know how she was looking—not suggested
going to a restaurant. In this state!

Calm down, Marnie, and be thankful that nobody saw you on the stairs. Relax in a soothing bath and forget about the paperwork for tonight.

The paperwork! Where was her briefcase? She'd had it when she left—yes, definitely. But had she dropped it in the street when she ran, left it at the lodge, or in James's car? She drew a blank at the police station and the hospital, and, when she got James's answering machine, she hung up before the recorded message was finished. What had been in the case anyway—apart from her knitting? Her report for the next heads of department meeting and a rough draft of a hand-out for interested pupils at the Academy careers seminar. She'd have liked to do some more work on that, but it was already nearly ten. One forgot the time in the long light of summer.

Next morning, Marnie did something she'd never done before; she overslept. But then last night she'd done something else she'd never done before. To calm her jangled nerves, she'd drunk a double brandy before going to sleep.

It was the phone that woke her. She stumbled out of bed and went, blinking, to answer it, finding that it wasn't the actual phone, but the entryphone. What on earth. . .?

'Taxi for Miss Fraser-Firth,' assailed her ear in the richest of Duntrune accents.

'But I haven't—didn't. . .' But Marnie was coming to now. 'Who's that?' she demanded suspiciously, though pretty sure she could guess.

'Nobody can fool you for long can they?' asked James with a theatrical sigh. 'I just thought you'd like a lift to work as you've not got your car.'

'What's the time?' she asked, beginning to panic.

'Almost seven forty-five, so——'

'Oh, no!' she wailed. 'And I'm not even dressed!'

'How very convenient,' he purred. 'I'll be right up.'

'Don't bother—I'll get the bus,' she retorted quickly, hanging up without pressing the door release button. She regretted not being more gracious in refusing his offer, but that last remark had thrown her completely. A girl ought not to have to deal with a James Dalgleish before she was fully awake and tuned up for the day.

She had got as far as bra and pants when the doorbell rang twice. She dragged on her bathrobe and hurried to the door to see what the postman had brought her.

But it was James standing there, looking cool, poised and businesslike in one of his conventional dark consultant suits. 'How did you get in?' she asked faintly.

'Are you saying you didn't press the buzzer, then? How very ungrateful! It was a good thing the milkman was just coming out.' When she didn't stir, he slithered past her into the hall. 'If it's not too much trouble, I'd appreciate it if you'd speed up a little. I've got a heavy theatre list today and I'm making an early start.'

'I did say I'd get the bus. . .'

'I know, but you're not very good at catching buses, are you?'

Marnie fled to her bedroom, wishing she could lock the door and straight away thinking how silly that was when James was obviously in a hurry. She splashed cold water on her face, then flung on a clean blouse and yesterday's suit. She stuffed some tights in her bag, because if she tried to put them on now she'd certainly ladder them. Next she dragged a brush through her curls, waved the mascara wand in the general direction of her thick, gold-tipped lashes and stepped out into the hall. It was empty. 'Where are you?' she called.

'In the kitchen,' James called back. 'That was quick,'

he said approvingly when he saw her. 'The kettle's only just boiled.'

'What—why——?' she began.

'I expect it was because I switched it on,' he explained with maddening simplicity. 'Sit down.'

'But you're in a hurry.'

'It'll take you about five minutes to eat that——' a bowl of muesli, already milked '—and drink this.' The mug of black coffee he was putting down on the table in front of her. How did he know she liked it black? 'Mind if I have one too?'

'Help yourself,' she said indistinctly through her first mouthful. Why am I doing this? she thought. Why am I letting him order me about like this in my own home? Am I losing my grip?

'Nice place you've got here,' James said next. 'I suppose your father bought it for you.'

'No, my grandfather.'

'The retired baker of biscuits to the nation?' He gave her a speculative look. 'You must be a rich heiress.'

'Wrong. It's my cousin Fran you should be chatting up. Her father is the eldest son, not mine.'

'No, thanks, I'd rather die a pauper,' retorted James. 'I've known Fran since I was six. She's bossy and she's rude and her front teeth stick out. She's quite like you, in fact—except for the teeth.'

Marnie choked on her last spoonful of muesli, and James patted her vigorously on the back, increasing her distress. 'Sorry, was I not doing that right?' he asked when her coughing had subsided.

'Let me put it this way,' she said, wiping her eyes on her napkin. 'I think you should stick to surgery and forget physio.'

'Speaking of which——'

'Ready when you are.'

'Come on, then—but don't forget to lock up.'

'I'll not do that. This *is* my flat.' Marnie had wondered, though, during that last confusing ten minutes.

'Eight twenty-three; not bad in the circumstances,'
remarked James in a satisfied tone as the powerful car
purred through the hospital gates. 'I do like to be in
before the registrars. It keeps 'em on their toes.'

'I'm usually here before this too,' Marnie assured
him.

'You would be,' he said. 'But then I've nothing to
prove.'

'And just what did you mean by that remark?'
demanded Marnie haughtily when they were out of the
car and facing one another across its roof.

'I really don't know,' he answered infuriatingly. 'It
just sort of slipped out—though not without good
reason, I suspect.'

'I never knew anybody so skilful at wriggling off the
hook as you are, James Dalgleish,' retorted Marnie,
stalking off across the car park with what she hoped
was dignity. And she'd meant to thank him so grace-
fully for making her breakfast and bringing her to
work.

Sonia was waiting for her at the door of Physiotherapy. 'Whatever's wrong, love?' she asked
anxiously. 'You've been crying—I can tell.'

'Crying? Nonsense!' Marnie detoured into the
patients' loo to borrow a mirror. With mascara everywhere but where it should be, she looked almost as
messy as she had last night. 'I choked on breakfast,
which made my eyes water. Then, being in a hurry, I
never checked to see what that had done to my face.'

'But why?' asked Sonia. 'Hurry, I mean. You're here
in plenty of time.'

'Yes, but I wouldn't have been if I hadn't hurried.'

Sonia followed her into the office. 'I'm getting worried about you,' she said. 'You've always been conscientious, but lately you seem to be getting obsessional. When are you going to take a holiday?'

'Oh, the autumn, I should think. Look, Sonia, I appreciate your concern, but I'm fine—honestly. Or rather I will be when I've done something about my face. I look a real clown, do I not?'

'I've seen you looking better,' Sonia was saying as the phone rang on the desk.

Marnie picked it up, listened, looking rueful, and then turned to her friend. 'That was Jane. Her bus has broken down and they're waiting for a replacement, so she's going to be late. I'm afraid that means I'll have to hang on here to see to her outpatients, but I'll come up as soon as I can.'

'Thanks, Marnie, I know you will. But a bus breakdown, eh? That's a new one,' said Sonia as she departed.

In a clean uniform, her make-up immaculate and her blonde curls practically but becomingly restrained, Marnie stepped out into the corridor feeling much more like herself. Jane arrived about an hour later and Marnie was able to join Sonia, happy in the knowledge that James would now be safely shut up in Theatre and therefore unable to cause her any further aggravation that morning. Certainly he wasn't there in person, but she couldn't have been more wrong about the aggravation.

Marnie didn't take personally the giggles of the two young nurses who passed her in Ortho's main corridor, but Sonia's knowing smirk was another matter. 'Well, well, well—just fancy,' she said when Marnie walked into the office.

Marnie didn't get it at first, because Sonia had got

some X-rays up on the viewing screen and she assumed
Sonia must be referring to them. She peered over her
friend's shoulder. The pre-op films were a mess; the
tibia acutely angled at the fracture site, badly frag-
mented and obviously compound. The post-op X-ray,
by contrast, didn't seem to relate to the same leg. The
tibia was now in perfect alignment and its pieces neatly
held together with the minimum of metal. 'That's
certainly a nice result,' she remarked, 'but nothing
new. James Dalgleish certainly knows his job.'

'You've changed your tune,' Sonia said slyly.

Marnie's violet eyes widened with genuine innocence. 'What's that supposed to mean?' she asked. 'I
may deplore his lifestyle, but I've never denied his
skill. The wretch is a wonderful surgeon.'

'And an even more wonderful rescuer of damsels in
distress, I understand,' returned Sonia with barely
concealed amusement.

Marnie felt a tiny prickle of foreboding, but she went
on playing the innocent. 'Don't you really mean the
exact opposite?' she asked lightly. 'Think of our poor
little Fiona. Would you like me to take the men's class
again today?'

'I'd love it, but as it's all round the hospital, they've
probably heard too. Do you think you can take it?'

'Take what? Sonia, do we really have time for this?'

'No, but you'd better listen. In a nutshell, the place
is buzzing with the tale of how James the Lad fought
off two thugs who tried to kidnap you outside the gates
last night and then whisked you off in his car. As he
brought you in this morning, wearing the same clothes
and looking anything but your usual model self, they're
naturally drawing the most interesting conclusion.'

'I never heard such a travesty of fact in all my life!'
snorted Marnie indignantly. 'I'll sue that gate porter!'

'Actually, it was Staff Bell who told me,' corrected Sonia.

'Her and all, then,' threatened Marnie, her grammar going to pot under such stress. 'I'll set you straight at lunchtime, my girl, and then you can sort her—and anybody else who needs it. But now let's get to work.'

'Certainly.' A pause. 'Which ward would you like, Marnie?' asked Sonia, suspiciously meek.

'I—I think I'll take the women. After all, I do know them best.'

In view of the scurrilous rumours circulating, Marnie decided to leave Jinty and Judy till last, knowing she could count on some snide remarks from them. Time enough to cope then, when she could beat a hasty retreat when lunch was brought round. She began with the patient whose X-rays she'd just seen. 'How are you feeling now, Mrs Stewart?' she asked.

'Not today, thank you, dear,' returned the patient, just as though Marnie was the milkman or the Avon lady.

'You're in pain,' guessed Marnie sympathetically.

'Not at the moment, but I surely will be if you make me move.'

Patiently, Marnie explained the importance of moving all the joints you could when you had a long plaster on your leg. 'Toes first, please. No, not just a wiggle, but a real good bender.'

That usually got a stock response, and did so now. 'Sounds as if you're wanting to get me drunk,' obliged the patient, smiling.

'That didn't hurt, did it? Now for your hip. I'll take the weight—that's the ticket, and now if you could just sort of get the feeling that you're pressing your knee down inside the stookie. Great! Honestly, Mrs Stewart, you'll be glad we did all this when you try the crutches later on.'

'But I'm not to get up for a week,' Mrs Stewart told Marnie firmly.

Marnie didn't quite believe that, but she answered, 'All the more important to keep doing the exercises, then.'

'You lot have got an answer for everything,' sighed the patient.

'All part of the training, Mrs Stewart.'

Next, Marnie looked round for the double act of Troy and Anderson, but they had been transferred to the convalescent hospital, along with Mrs King. She just managed not to catch Jinty's eye and turned to one of last week's hip replacements. 'Hello, there, Mrs Melrose. Care for some exercises?'

'Just you try and stop me, hen!'

One of Andrew Wilkie's patients had a stitch abscess. 'Does Sister know about this?' Marnie asked a passing nurse.

'Yes, Miss Firth, and the registrar's been sent for.'

On with the round, coaxing, encouraging, answering questions and exchanging jokes. Only Jinty and Judy left now.

'Well, well, well!' opened Jinty.

'Yes, very well indeed, thank you,' returned Marnie coolly, thinking how smart she'd been to come up with that.

The two of them went into giggles. 'I'll bet,' sniggered Jinty. 'So would I be—after a night with his nibs!'

Marnie put on an innocent look at odds with the colour of her cheeks. 'I was working last night,' she retorted loftily. 'So I was unable to meet my boyfriend after all.'

'Will ye listen to her!' crowed Jinty. 'Work, she calls it!'

'Must be moonlighting, then,' was Judy's contribution. 'I wish I'd done physiotherapy instead of maths—the overtime sounds much more interesting.' And off they went again. If nothing else, Marnie's predicament had brought Judy out of her depression.

The arrival of Sister and the registrar to see the patient with the abscess provided temporary relief, and Marnie got swiftly to work. Before the registrar left, Andrew Wilkie was in the ward, providing a further check on the two comediennes. When Andrew left, so did Marnie, and before the girls could draw breath to start again.

Over sandwiches in her office, Marnie gave Sonia the correct version of the night's happenings. 'And now I'm relying on you to set the record straight,' she said.

Sonia promised to do her best, but wasn't hopeful. 'You know what folk are,' she said. 'And as the truth's not nearly as interesting, I'm afraid they'll prefer the other version. But never mind, love. The ones who really know you will never believe such a tale.'

Marnie hoped Sonia was right, and resolved to put the problem out of her mind while she got on with her afternoon.

Her outpatients first and then a talk to student nurses about how to avoid back strain when lifting. After that came a long, boring and, to Marnie's mind, a time-wasting heads of department meeting. Whatever the agenda, and it was usually trivial, such meetings always seemed to degenerate into a general grumble.

Apart from the head porter hoping, with a distinct gleam in his one good eye, that her car was running well again, nothing was said to indicate that yesterday's

adventures had aroused any interest. So it was a pity
that they should all be coming out of the committee-
room just as James came swinging down the corridor,
carrying Marnie's briefcase. Surely he'd have more tact
than to raise the matter now?

He hadn't. 'Yours, I believe, Miss Fraser-Firth.' He
never failed to give her both barrels in public.

'Yes indeed, Mr Dalgleish. Thank you so much.
Wherever did you find it?' Now there was a daft
question, when the last thing she wanted was for him
to tell her in front of this lot! And did she really think
that trying to sound like a Jane Austen heroine was
going to fool anybody? Marnie signalled desperately
with her eyebrows.

'Have you got something in your eye?' James
enquired wickedly. 'Come over to this window and I'll
take a look.'

Well, at least she'd got him off the subject of the
briefcase. 'I'm not sure—something's irritating. . .
And if you say one word out of place, I'll kill you!' she
hissed under cover of the examination.

He had the sense to wait until the party had dispersed
before asking with a broad grin and undeniable relish,
'Did you know it's all round the hospital that we spent
last night together?'

Marnie gave him her snootiest look. 'I did—and a
more unlikely pairing I never heard of. Nobody sensible could possibly believe it.'

'The circumstantial evidence is very strong,' James
pointed out provokingly.

'Rubbish! My girls know the truth of the matter and
have been setting people straight all afternoon.' I hope!
'I'm quite sure that——'

'Not ten minutes since, Robert Leith told me in his
best kirk elder manner that he hopes I mean to make

an honest woman of you,' James interrupted with a look that would not have disgraced an angel.

Dr Leith—senior physician at the hospital and a lifelong friend of her father's! Thank God Dad was away on that lecture tour! But perhaps James had made that up. 'I don't believe you!' she exclaimed. But then again, perhaps he hadn't. 'Did he really say that— exactly?' Marnie asked anxiously next minute.

'Not in just those words, perhaps—but that was the gist of it.'

'I knew that couldn't be true. You're enough to give a girl heart failure! And don't pretend to misunderstand that!'

From further down the corridor came the sound of muffled laughter and scurrying feet as a class of student nurses poured out of the lecture theatre.

'Thanks for returning my briefcase,' said Marnie hurriedly, already walking away.

'Who is it for, Marnie?' James called after her.

She paused. 'What? I don't understand.'

'That baby's jacket you're making.'

Not even he would have opened her case deliberately, so those weak clasps must have given way again. Marnie was colouring as though caught out in cruelty rather than an act of kindness. 'It's for Lynne Selkirk's new arrival. I always make something for my girls' babies.'

'You old softie,' said James indulgently. 'We'll make a woman of you yet.'

Marnie was glad he walked away immediately. No way could she have come up with a one-liner to beat that. It rankled, though, the knowledge that any man— even such a one as he—could think she wasn't all woman already.

CHAPTER FOUR

NEXT morning, with the most pressing admin chores dealt with, Marnie was just setting out for Ortho-paedics when Belle came running after her to say that Betty had called in sick. 'Yet *another* tummy bug,' she added scathingly.

'Damn!' said Marnie. This was the fourth time in the last two months, and always on a Monday or a Friday. Belle wasn't the only one with doubts about Betty's frequent weekend afflictions. But Marnie didn't waste time bewailing. 'Right! I'll treat her outpatients and take her antenatal class. Be a dear please, Belle, and ring Sonia to say I can't make it this morning.'

'And then I s'pose I'd better cancel as many of Betty's p.m. patients as I can get hold of,' said Belle, who was getting used to this. 'You'll certainly want to get to the wards some time today.'

Marnie asked what in the world she'd do without Belle, and Belle said that was the sixty-four-thousand-dollar question.

The aggro went on all morning. No sooner had Marnie begun a treatment than she was called away; to the phone, to advise one of her younger therapists, or to placate a patient who thought she'd missed her turn.

'This reminds me of last year, when they tried to do a time and motion study on me,' she told Sonia when the two of them met as usual for a hurried snack in her office at lunchtime. 'The only positive thing they came up with was that eight and a half minutes was the longest I'd gone all week without being interrupted.

60

And then the poor little T and M man went off sick with a nervous breakdown. But never mind my woes. How did you get on this morning without my help?'

'As well as could be expected,' Sonia answered philosophically. 'But James the Lad was quite put out when he found you'd deserted him, as he put it.'

'What rubbish that man does talk! He knows fine I'm only helping out when I can. And why!'

'You mean you actually tackled him about Fiona?' Sonia was fascinated. 'Whatever did you say?'

'Not half as much as I'd have liked to, though I did tell him she'd gone missing,' said Marnie.

'Losh, that should have put the breeze up him. What did he say to that?'

'That Fiona was rather a sweet wee thing, but immature—and, if she wasn't just playing truant, shouldn't I call the police?'

'Oh, very cool,' considered Sonia.

'Callous, more like,' Marnie was saying when a brisk tap on the door was swiftly followed up by the entry of the man himself.

'Who's callous?' he asked curiously.

'Far too many people, in my opinion,' Marnie returned with great presence of mind, 'but Sonia and I were discussing a—patient's foot, as it happens.'

At that, Sonia rushed out with her hankie over her mouth, as James said, 'What a delightful topic for the lunch-hour!' He peered at the label on Marnie's sandwich packet. 'Prawn mayonnaise—how wonderful! Are you going to eat them both?'

'That was the general idea. Why? Do you think I'm putting on weight or something?' What a wonderful chance for him to give her a close scan.

James didn't waste it. 'Everything's quite perfect as far as I can see,' he assured her, sitting down in Sonia's chair and swinging his long legs up on the desk. 'I only asked because I'm off to Theatre in approximately ten minutes, so I've no time to go to the canteen. And it's going to be a long session too,' he went on pathetically. 'A below-knee amputation and two necks of femur for pinning and plating. Not to mention a change of plaster for Fred Mackeson. His present one is smelling the ward out.'

'An even more unsuitable topic for lunchtime conversation,' observed Marnie, who by now was looking quite green. 'Oh, go on, then—eat the lot, why don't you? You've put me right off, as you no doubt intended. And you may as well drink my coffee too.' She pushed it across the desk to him, along with a packet of chocolate biscuits.

'You can be quite enchanting when you choose,' he told her with an engaging grin she fought to ignore. Then just as he was about to take his first bite he said remorsefully, 'I'm sorry, Marnie. You never could stand Theatre, could you? I've just remembered that time you fainted right in the middle of a laminectomy and had to be carried out. You'd be in your second student year, I should think. Old Ferguson said in that dry way of his, "That girl is certainly not a chip off the old block", and calmly went on dissecting.' It had been a perfect take-off of a revered surgeon, now retired.

Marnie stared at him, open-mouthed. 'Were you there? I didn't see you.'

'When did you ever?' he asked whimsically. 'But I was there, newly promoted to SHO and ready to save the world—or at least that bit of it called Duntrune. I suppose that's why you did physio instead of medicine. You'd never have stood the compulsory stint on surgery.'

'That was part of it,' Marnie agreed, amazed at both

his memory and his understanding of a weakness she'd always been rather ashamed of and had thought she'd managed to keep a secret. 'I think it began the day I found some specimens in my father's study,' she found herself confessing. 'They looked absolutely revolting, and, thinking I was interested, he insisted on telling me all about them. I had nightmares for weeks! I was only nine.'

'You poor wee thing,' he said warmly.

Similar words to those he'd used to describe Fiona—and just what was needed to jolt Marnie out of this silly mood. 'Quite. But I don't imagine you came here to reminisce and steal my lunch, so what did bring you?'

James winced visibly at her abrupt change of tone before saying quietly, 'I was wondering if you'd consider taking the medical students on permanently. Word has gone round that you're much more interesting and well informed than poor old Emily.'

'Oh, dear—she'll be devastated if she's dropped.'

'I can't help that, Marnie. She's losing her grip as well as being miles behind the times. And there's talk of mutiny, if the change isn't made.'

'You're putting me in a very awkward position,' she said. 'Emily will cut me dead in future if I agree. And yet. . .'

'It's the perfect chance to get your views across—and get them pro-physio from the start. Surely that can't be bad?' He looked at his watch before starting on the last sandwich.

'I'll think about it,' Marnie promised. 'I'll talk to Emily, and if she doesn't mind too much, then—perhaps. . .'

'She'd better not,' he said getting up and taking a biscuit. 'To eat on the way,' he explained. 'Thanks for the splendid lunch, Marnie—and thanks for agreeing. You're a girl in a million! See you!' And he was away in his usual whirlwind fashion.

Marnie sat back, feeling as though she'd just been run over by a steamroller. Come to think of it, most encounters over the years with James Dalgleish had left her feeling like this. *Has anybody ever got him on the ropes, I wonder? I didn't agree—I only said I'd think about it. And damn the man—I'm feeling quite hungry now!*

'Pity about that,' said Sonia as the two girls walked up to Ortho soon afterwards.

'Pity about what?' asked Marnie.

'James the Lad coming in like that. Not the best way of reinforcing that tale we gave to the staff yesterday, was it?'

'And what's so strange about a consultant looking in at lunchtime?' demanded Marnie. 'They often do. They've got the time then and they can be pretty sure of catching me. And that wasn't a tale, it was the plain unvarnished truth.'

'I know that—there's no need to get so uptight! I only meant it was a pity he decided to come calling right on top of the latest grapevine sensation.'

'The girls know me,' insisted Marnie.

'Sure they do. But one or two have been heard to say they wouldn't mind being in your shoes.'

'I hope you came down like a ton of bricks on such silly talk,' said Marnie crossly.

'No, I did not. Overreacting is no way to take the heat out of the situation.'

Sonia was, of course, quite right. *Keep the heid, Marnie. Laugh off any hints you can't ignore and keep out of James's way as much as possible. He'll soon get* tired of baiting you and then the rumour will die a natural death.

Keeping out of James's way was no problem that afternoon with him in Theatre, and, as Sister was in the ward nearly all the time Marnie was treating Jinty and Judy, the aggro from that quarter was minimal. Apart from helping Sonia to get Basher up on his crutches, she kept away from the men.

At half-past five, Marnie retired thankfully to her office, kicked off her shoes and settled down to some correspondence. There wasn't much, but she meant to make it last until the window cleaners had finished. Last month, they had missed all the windows on the east side. The letters done, Marnie looked at the desk pad to see if there was anything she'd overlooked. Of course! The sessions for the medical students. She reached for the directory and then phoned Emily at home.

'Who? Marnie Firth? Could this not have waited? I was just feeding my pussy.'

Six little words that summed up Emily's bleak existence in the neat suburban villa she had inherited from her parents. Marnie had a fleeting glimpse of herself in thirty years' time, unless. . . She pulled her thoughts back on course, but found she couldn't broach the subject in case Emily was hurt. So she said she'd only called to see how Emily was feeling.

'That's very kind of you, Marnie,' returned Emily in a noticeably warmer tone. 'And actually, I'm very glad you've called. There's something I've been wanting to ask you. A favour. . .'

'Ask away,' said Marnie, who found it much easier to oblige folk than to deal them blows.

'As you know, I've been ordered to rest, and as you've already stood in for me on one occasion with the medical students, I was wondering if you'd consider finishing the series.'

Careful, Marnie, don't sound too keen. . . 'I'm quite busy myself, Emily, but I could probably fit it all in—with a bit of juggling.'

Emily said she'd be eternally grateful, so when Marnie rang off she wrote a note to James, telling him the matter had been resolved without any hurt feelings. She put it in the internal mail tray, and as there wasn't time to go home first, she took a shower in the changing-room and then spruced herself up to go and meet Dominic.

As she crossed the car park, she noticed that the lights were still on in the orthopaedic theatre. James had been right in his estimate of that session. He'd needed her lunch more than she had after all.

The evening at the opera followed the usual unde-manding course Marnie had come to expect with Dominic—the Continental kisses on both cheeks at meeting, mutual enjoyment of the performance and intelligent discussion of the singing during the intervals.

'And now for a little light supper at Gigli's, dear,' said Dominic, gallantly offering his arm for support as they crossed the road to the restaurant which drew so much of its late-night trade from theatregoers.

Marnie let him choose because it pleased him, and anyway, he knew her tastes. Later, over coffee, she asked, 'Will I see you this weekend, dear?'

'Sorry, dear, but I'll be out of town. The chairman is having a get-together at his lodge in Glen Lyon. Negotiations with Kleinson are reaching a critical stage.'

'But you'll succeed,' supposed Marnie confidently.

'Oh, indubitably.' He can be so pedantic sometimes, Marnie caught herself thinking, as she stifled a yawn.

'Tired, dear?' queried Dominic.

'Just a bit. It's been a helluva day.'

Dominic frowned ever so slightly at her description. 'You work too hard,' he considered. 'You should cut down a bit.'

'There's not much chance of that in hospital. Our workload is of necessity erratic.'

'Nonsense! All that's needed is good organisation and forward planning,' stated Dominic as he snapped his fingers for the waiter to bring the bill.

Tell that to accident victims, thought Marnie, as she opened her bag to give him her share.

But tonight Dominic waved her contribution aside. 'No, no—this is on me, dear.'

That meant he was feeling like some decorous snogging—a mood brought on by the sensuous music of *Traviata*, no doubt.

And so it proved. Marnie participated with equal decorum. After all, this was all a part of life's rich tapestry, was it not?

Next morning, she spent some time deciding what to wear. It had to be something that would impress the careers adviser at Duntrune Academy, yet festive enough for the hospital fête in the afternoon. She settled on a suit in shades of pink, blue and violet flowered cotton, with short sleeves and a longish flared skirt.

The session at the school turned out to be a pleasure, with two strong probables among the enquirers. Now there was just time to pop into the nearest pub for a ploughman's, before making her way to the convalescent hospital on the city's outskirts, where the fête was

always held. There wasn't an inch of grass left anywhere at the main hospital. Even the tennis courts had
been built on long ago.

The Royal Infirmary's annual summer fête was a
leftover from pre-NHS days, when it had raised most
of the money the hospital needed. It was still a fund-
raiser, but now it was run by the League of Friends
and the money went to whichever speciality was most
in need of it. This year they were aiming to buy a body
scanner, so that patients need not be shuttled back and
forth to the Western General Hospital.

Woe betide any off-duty member of staff who failed
to attend, and as the fête was cunningly timed to
coincide with the start of the city's annual summer
holiday fortnight there was also maximum support from
the inhabitants as well. The glorious weather had
ensured a better than usual turn-out, and with the
official car park already full Marnie had to park in a
side-street. She was just in time to hear the Lord
Provost declare the fête open, before hurrying to the
exhibition tent, where each department had a small
display, intended to show something of their work to
the uninitiated. As she had had a date the night before,
Sonia had supervised the setting up, and now Marnie
was to do her bit by taking the first hour of duty.

Nobody was bothered with indoor attractions on
such a lovely day, and, after an hour of boredom,
Marnie was glad to hand over to Jane and wander out
into the sunshine. There were sideshows, a fair for the
children, pony rides, a dog show and any number of
competitions and races; also a small tented shopping
mall, where Duntrune's leading shops exhibited their
wares—and paid dearly for the privilege.

Just about the first person Marnie saw was James
Dalgleish. At once she turned to run, caught her foot

in a guy rope and fell headlong. Somebody picked her up, and she knew by his chuckle who it was. 'Thank you, but you can let me go now,' she said graciously. 'I can stand on my own two feet.'

'If you say so, but on recent evidence. . .' James let that sink in before releasing her. 'Did you hurt yourself?'

'No—thank you.'

'You deserved to, running away like that. Why did you?'

'Because it would never do for us to be seen talking together like this. Such rotten luck!' she added.

'Luck had nothing to do with it. Sonia told me you were taking the two-to-three stint at the physio stand, so all I had to do was wait for you to come out.'

Just wait until I get my hands on you, Sonia Graham! she thought. 'That was enterprising of you, but don't expect a medal for it,' she told him.

'One of your twice-yearly smiles would be enough,' said James. His eyes travelled down to her slim ankles. 'Did you know you've torn your tights?'

'No, but I'm not surprised,' she returned bitterly. 'Oh lord, there's Robert Leith! Where can I hide?'

'Allow me,' said James, stepping gallantly in front of her. 'It's all right, he's gone inside,' he reported a moment later. Then, tucking her arm under his, he led her towards the shops.

'Please let me go, James,' she pleaded. 'Somebody might see us.'

'By that, I presume you mean somebody who knows us. So what? They'll only see what they expect to see— in view of a certain story currently going the rounds.'

'A story that would die a natural death if it were allowed to.' Marnie decided to appeal to his common sense. 'Look, James, you must be as embarrassed by

all this nonsense as I am.' Even as she spoke, she
realised how unlikely that was, or he'd not have come
looking for her.

'I'm not in the least embarrassed,' he returned,
predictably. 'On the contrary, I find the situation
quite—piquant.'

Piquant indeed! 'All right, so you're not embarrassed, but I am. I appeal to your sense of honour.'

To Marnie's dismay, James went off into peals of
laughter. 'Coming as it does from the girl who's always
made it plain she doesn't believe I have such a thing,
that's really rich!' he crowed when he'd recovered
enough. 'Now come along, there's a good girl. It's my
fault your tights are torn, so now I'm taking you
shopping.' And with that, he thrust her into Duntrune's
mobile equivalent of Harrods. 'My young lady has had
a nasty fall and needs some tights,' he told the assistant.

'Oh, dear, I'm sorry to hear that, sir,' said the girl,
looking sympathetic. 'Has she seen a doctor? I should
think you'll find one easily enough at this do.'

'That's a very good suggestion,' said James, poker-
faced. 'We'll certainly act on it. What size do you take,
dear?' he enquired tenderly of Marnie, who was now
fighting a strong desire to giggle.

'They're all one size,' explained the helpful assistant,
dragging packets out of a rack.

'How practical,' said James, choosing the most
expensive pair. 'Will it be all right if she changes
behind that rail of sweaters?'

'Of course,' said the girl, and, before she knew it,
Marnie was wearing her new tights.

Standing up to James Dalgleish was about as effec-
tive as King Canute attempting to stop the incoming
tide, but Marnie felt she simply must go on trying.
When they left the little booth, she said, 'That was

really kind and thoughtful of you, James, but now we'll call a halt to this, if you please. In any case, I have to leave soon.'

'Oh, look!' he exclaimed. 'Here come the Wilkies. Smile nicely now.'

After a few minutes' conversation with the senior orthopaedic surgeon and his wife which could hardly be avoided, Marnie renewed her efforts to get through to James.

'You're very ungrateful,' he told her. 'I'm only trying to help, but if you really prefer to be seen as a one-night stand then have it your way.'

That brought Marnie up short, and she stared up at him aghast for several seconds before saying uneasily, 'You're joking. Nobody who knows me really believes that scurrilous version of things.'

'Don't be so naïve,' he said. 'There's nothing folk enjoy more than a nice scandal. Especially those who rather envy your cool superiority—pride taking a fall and all that. Sorry, Marnie, but that really is how some people see you. But play this my way and you can salvage your precious pride. Let's spend some time together and make sure that the grapevine knows all about it. Then in a week or two—longer if necessary— we can cool it and let it be known you've dumped me. I don't mind; my back's broad enough.' He moved closer and added softly, 'On the other hand, you may discover you rather like the way things are going.'

'Why, you—you. . .!' began Marnie, breaking off abruptly as the senior nursing officer and her best friend the superintendent radiographer came into view. The looks they cast towards her were frankly disapproving, and it was galling.

'I expect they thought you were pleading with *me*

not to dump *you*,' said James, capitalising on that chance encounter.

Marnie feared that was all too likely. Neither was well disposed towards her, believing she was much too young to hold her post and had only got it through parental influence. And they certainly wouldn't be the only ones happy to believe the current scandal. 'A—a week or two, you said,' she whispered uncertainly. But was putting her head in the lion's mouth really the only way out?

'Or longer, if that's what it takes. You've nothing to lose.'

Only my reputation, and that's already in shreds anyway, she thought. 'Come on, let's get started, then,' Marnie said resignedly. 'The sooner we start this farce, the sooner we can end it.'

'I could wish you'd phrased that more gratefully,' said James, 'but I'm glad you're seeing sense.' And with that, he tucked her arm under his once more and led her out to face the crowds.

It was certainly a convincing parade of unity—he made sure of that. There was hardly a hospital worker there who didn't see them together. Having tea, judging the bouncing baby competition, at the coconut shy, sharing an ice-cream cornet—very Freudian, that! When the crowds began to thin out as people drifted away, James said they might as well leave too.

Marnie replied firmly that perhaps this was all that was required. She had to say that. She'd enjoyed her afternoon so much that she was seriously worried about becoming addicted.

'Nonsense!' James declared even more firmly. 'This is only the beginning. Where would you like to go for dinner?'

Marnie squashed a deplorable thrill of anticipation

to ask practically, 'Is there any need to go to such lengths unless we can be sure of being seen?'

'That's a very good question, so let me think. Hugh Reid always takes his missus to the Golden Cockerel on his Saturday nights off, but he's on call this weekend.' He snapped his fingers. 'I know—we'll drive out to the Riverside Inn at Invertrune. I overheard Jack Marshall telling Theatre Sister he's going there tonight for some sort of family celebration.'

'You do have such useful contacts,' said Marnie with an irony which was quite lost on him.

'That's true, and will make our campaign easier to plan.'

'Of course, the Riverside may already be fully booked,' Marnie pointed out.

'Kindly do not look for trouble, or I may think you're not as bothered about your reputation as I am. Where's your car?'

'About four blocks away.'

'Come on then, I'll walk you there. It's always another opportunity for exposure.'

'Why else?' asked Marnie.

'Wear something sexy,' James had said at parting, but Marnie wasn't about to go over the top. Besides, she doubted that she owned a dress which would conform to that definition in his opinion. When in doubt, wear black, her mother always used to tell her, so after a nice cool shower and plenty of Ma Griffe eau-de-toilette, Marnie shrugged herself into a neat black sheath cut down to the waist at the back, but collar-bone-high at the front. The low back meant she couldn't wear a bra, but her breasts were firm enough to cope on their own, now and again.

When she opened the door to James, he didn't speak

at once, just stood there and stared. 'You really are— utterly fabulous,' he said slowly at last.

Marnie was glad her dress wasn't too tight in the bodice, or he would have seen her heart beating twice as fast as it ought. 'I do my best,' she responded lightly. He was looking fairly stupendous himself in a white dinner-jacket.

'Even your worst leaves all the other girls way behind,' he considered.

Marnie stepped out on to the landing, looking to right and left. 'You're being very thorough, considering there isn't a single solitary person in sight,' she commented drily.

'I have to practise,' said James. 'After all, Andrew Wilkie lives across the landing.' He slid his arm around her waist. 'Shall I kiss you, in case he opens his door?' he suggested softly.

'Thanks, but there's no need to put yourself to that trouble,' said Marnie, slipping cleverly out of his grasp. 'I heard Andrew and Susan going out quite half an hour ago.' She locked the door and dropped the key in her bag. 'So let the grand deception begin.'

'I rather thought it had already,' said James as they clattered down the stairs.

The Riverside was new to Marnie; Dominic having always vetoed it on the grounds that it was grossly overpriced. It was certainly expensive, but the food was perfect, as was the wine and the décor.

James made sure that Jack Marshall and his party saw them, by stopping by their table to make a few witty remarks with James's arm around Marnie's shoulders all the time. 'What luck the McPhees were there too,' he exulted as they left. 'Amy McPhee is the most dedicated gossip going. She'll have rung up all the consultants' wives by lunchtime tomorrow.'

'Ah!' said Marnie thoughtfully.

'What's the matter with you now?' demanded James. 'Is that not coverage enough—for starters?'

Marnie had agreed to this madness in a weak moment, right after that put-down by the senior nursing officer and her friend. But after that meeting with those surgeons and their wives she was rattled. Her father might be on the other side of the Atlantic just now, but supposing he got to hear of this? 'I was actually wondering if it might not have been too much,' she admitted.

'Impossible!' declared James, opening the door of his car for her. 'We're playing for high stakes, remember.'

Marnie watched him stride round to the other side and put a hand over her fast-beating heart. Play, he had said. I mustn't forget this is all a game, she thought as they headed for home.

With that in mind, she told James not to bother coming up to the flat with her. 'And I don't see why you should have all the expense either,' she added, opening her bag.

When he saw what she was about, he took the bag out of her hands and closed it firmly. 'Havers!' was all he had to say about that. 'And as to not coming up, I have to,' he said. 'You see, I've had this wonderful idea. I'm going to walk home and leave my car here all night, to impress Andrew.'

'Don't you dare!' she protested. 'He's a pillar of the kirk, remember—just like Robert Leith—and impressed is the last thing he'd be. But thanks for tonight, James. It was great fun, as well as being useful. . .' She was talking to herself. James had got out and was walking towards the entrance, still carrying her bag.

'Oh, lord, what have I started?' groaned Marnie, getting out and going after him. 'You didn't lock the car,' she said.

James turned round and held out the key. 'Remote control,' he said laconically. 'Which of these keys is for the outside door, dear? It's looking like rain.' He'd had the nerve to take them out of her bag!

James had drunk sparingly at dinner, but then he always did—Marnie knew that—so she wasn't surprised that he refused the brandy she offered when he had unlocked the door and ushered her into her own flat. 'Coffee, then?' she suggested. 'A grateful patient gave me a pound of best Blue Mountain beans just the other day.' If she didn't get a glass or a cup into his hand, he might decide to take hold of her, even though there was nobody to see and take note.

She'd read his intention aright. 'No brandy and no coffee—just this,' he said softly, pulling her gently towards him.

His hand on her back was electrifying, his other hand on her breast even more so. And when he kissed her, Marnie thought she'd faint. Nobody, but nobody had ever kissed her like this, and she was clutching at him, not from passion, but because she was buckling at the knees. At first, that was. It wasn't long before she was kissing him back in a way she hadn't known she knew.

'My God, Marnie, you're really something!' James breathed unsteadily. 'How could I ever have thought you cold?'

Marnie might be warming up in a way she'd never intended, but she retained enough sense not to burst into flame, so when he bent his head to kiss her again, she forced herself to turn away, presenting him with her ear. Then she tried to push him away. 'I think that'll do nicely for now,' she managed to say brightly. 'Andrew Wilkie may live across the landing, but he doesn't have X-ray eyes.'

She had expected a bit of a tussle, and was very surprised when James let her go at once. That simply wasn't in character. Then he raised a gentle hand and stroked her cheek, as though to assure himself that she was real. 'So where are we going tomorrow?' he asked huskily.

It was a relief to be able to say that tomorrow was already spoken for, because Marnie needed time to recover before exposing herself again to the full force of his attraction.

James frowned. 'Are you going out with another man?' he demanded.

'There'll be men there, yes.' She was going to a family gathering at her grandfather's house.

'More than one?' he pounced. 'A mixed party, then?'

'Yes. Why?'

'Because dating somebody else might send the wrong signals—if you were spotted,' explained James, sounding almost his usual jaunty self again.

'I never thought of that,' said Marnie, leading the way to the door.

'You couldn't run a kirk social, let alone an anti-gossip campaign,' James said tenderly, pulling her close and kissing her. 'Goodnight, then, you lovely, lovely thing. Promise to ring me tomorrow if you get home before midnight.'

'How will that help the campaign?' she wondered.

'I don't suppose it will, but it sure as hell will help me,' he said candidly, before helping himself to one last kiss.

Marnie shut the door on him and leaned against it,

one hand over her galloping heart. She was scared, really scared, at the strength of feeling he had awakened in her. 'I must have been out of my mind to agree to this,' she breathed.

CHAPTER FIVE

IT WAS a very different Marnie who rose early to shower and dress carefully for work on Monday morning. The repair had begun with a quiet family Sunday in the country, and afterwards a civilised unemotional phone chat with Dominic had completed it.

There was one slightly sticky moment when the phone rang again at two minutes to midnight. Marnie knew instinctively that if she picked it up she would hear James's deep, disturbing voice. She coped by not answering. When it rang again twenty minutes later, she wrapped it up in her thickest sweater and stuffed it in a cupboard. That way, she could hardly hear it at all. Then she unplugged the extension by her bed and slept until the radio switched itself on. Marnie the vulnerable woman had gone, and Marnie the cool, calm superintendent physiotherapist was back.

'Nice weekend, Marnie?' asked Andrew Wilkie curiously as they walked down the stairs together.

'On the whole it was, thank you, Andrew.' A sophisticated little laugh that came out just right. 'I could have done without the fête, but then couldn't we all? Only it's more than one's life is worth to miss that. But yesterday, out at Burnside with just the family, was wonderful. They certainly know how to enjoy life.' Marnie didn't recognise her relatives in the picture she was painting, but, as Andrew was looking suitably baffled, what did that matter?

'That's nice,' he observed feebly. 'I wish I could say the same, but I was on call.'

'Just as you were at Easter, I remember. You really
shouldn't let James Dalgleish get away with taking all
the holiday weekends off. It's not fair.' Was that last
bit over the top? worried Marnie as she went to get her
car. Still, at least she'd shown Andrew she wasn't
seriously involved with James. Now she must keep her
cool for taking it on the chin at the hospital.

She was seated at her desk and going through the
mail when Sonia poked her head round the office door.
'You made a fine spectacle of yourself on Saturday,'
she observed severely as she came in. 'What in the
world were you playing at?'

Marnie sighed. There were disadvantages in having
your best friend on your staff. 'That was James's idea,'
she explained. 'He suggested that we should make a—
a sort of parade and then put it about that I've dropped
him. To dispel the idea of a one-night stand, and save
my pride.'

'And you fell for it?' Sonia was looking quite
incredulous.

Marnie blinked. 'I don't know what you mean. I
thought it was rather generous of him. . .' She was
beginning to see how it looked to Sonia, and she didn't
much like what she saw. 'You think he's just taking me
for a ride, don't you?' she asked on a dying breath.

'What else? Oh, Marnie, how could you be so
naïve?'

'And it wasn't just the fête,' Marnie admitted, going
on to describe the dinner at the Riverside and James's
elaborate charade for the benefit of his colleagues and
their wives. 'What am I going to do, Sonia?' she asked
in a little voice. 'Amy McPhee will have told all the
consultants' wives by now.'

'After that, there's not much else you can do but go
along with it. But make sure you really are the one

who does the dropping. And make sure that everybody knows it. With luck, we could make it seem as if, all the time, you were only out to teach him a lesson.' Sonia warmed to her theme. 'Manage this properly and you could end up quite a heroine. When are you going out with him again?'

'I don't know.' Sonia looked anxious at that, so Marnie explained hurriedly about not being able to make yesterday and how she'd refused to answer the phone at night.

Sonia's expression relaxed. 'All right, but be sure to——' She broke off when Belle came in.

'Neither Betty nor Fiona is here yet,' Belle announced grimly.

'Damn!' exploded Marnie, her own concerns forgotten. 'Sorry, Sonia, I'll need to stay here and cover for Betty again, but I'll come up as soon as ever I can. I'm afraid that's the best I can do.'

'And a very good best too, in the circumstances.' Sonia was loyal as well as outspoken. 'And don't forget my advice,' she added before departing.

With Belle's help, Marnie got through the mail in record time and was ready and waiting when Betty's first patient came in. When she'd rung Betty's home number, there'd been no reply, so she knew how she would deal with her. But where was Fiona—and how would she react when she returned to find that her boss in a million was dating the man who had broken her heart? She'd never believe it had all come about so recently. Or why! 'I wish I was with Dad in America,' muttered Marnie as she bustled into cubicle six to fix up Mrs Watt on the traction table.

Mrs Watt was rather deaf. 'That must be awful nasty, dear,' she sympathised.

'What must be nasty, Mrs Watt?'

'Bad urticaria. Do you have something to put on it?'

I'm going mad, decided Marnie, until she made the connection. Never embarrass a patient if it can be avoided—or admit that you talk to yourself! 'That's a kind thought—I believe calamine lotion's as good as anything,' she returned. 'But your problem is the important one. I'd like to test your back movements before we give it that good stretch Mr Wilkie has asked for. Now then. . .'

It was well after one before Marnie was able to retire thankfully to her office with the intention of putting on the kettle for a coffee. She pulled up short in the doorway on seeing James sprawled lazily in her best chair with his feet on the desk, practically in the 'Out' tray. 'What the devil. . .!' she exclaimed.

James put on a wounded look. 'That's no way to greet the man in your life—especially after the tender way we parted on Saturday night,' he added with what Marnie could only think of as a leer. His manner wasn't tender but teasing today. Perhaps he regretted the line he'd taken then. Certainly he seemed to have forgotten asking her to ring.

Marnie slammed the door shut. 'Keep your voice down, you fool!' she hissed.

'Why?' he enquired. 'Are we not supposed to be in the middle of a steamy affair?'

'There's no need to—to go overboard. And who put that on?' she demanded when the kettle came to the boil.

'I did. Who else?' asked James, removing his feet from the desk and getting up in one continuous, lithe movement.

Marnie watched him make coffee in a small cafetière. 'And where did that come from?' she demanded.

'My office, but as we'll be lunching here together from now on——'

'Who says?'

James swung round to regard her provocatively. 'You're right, of course. Going to the canteen would provide much more exposure.'

'I can't believe this is really happening,' breathed Marnie, collapsing in the nearest chair and gazing up at him. 'Do you never listen to anything anybody says?'

'Not unless they're making sense, which you are not.'

'And you are, I suppose!'

'Certainly. We have an impression to give, remember? And right now you're making a very poor job of your role.'

'I wouldn't say that—not when we're shut up together in my office. What more could I do?' she demanded.

He chuckled deep in his throat. 'You might try a sexy little giggle or two—for the benefit of anybody passing,' he was suggesting as his bleep went off. He lifted the phone at once. 'Mr Dalgleish here. Who wants me?' His tone was brisk now and his expression intent as he listened.

'Campaign postponed for now,' he said briefly. 'There's been an accident down at the docks. See you!' He was away in a flash, leaving Marnie gazing after him with something very like disappointment.

There was a plastic carrier bag beside the cafetière, and Marnie went to investigate, finding sandwiches and fruit. She shrugged. James might have to forgo his lunch, but there was no reason why she should. As she munched, she tried to decide what she was going to do about him. No good idea had presented itself by the

time Sonia came to see if Marnie was going with her to
the wards.

Contrary to custom, Sonia knocked on the door and
waited for Marnie to open it. She peered over Marnie's
shoulder. 'He's gone, then,' she observed.

Marnie sighed. 'I might have known it was too much
to hope that little visit went unremarked. James dashed
off ages ago to an emergency.'

'The girls can talk of nothing else,' Sonia told her.

Marnie sighed some more. 'Tell me something I
couldn't have guessed,' she said.

'But I keep telling them you're only amusing
yourself.'

'Thanks, Sonia, you're a real pal,' said Marnie
gratefully.

'Mind you, they don't believe me,' Sonia added.

Marnie sighed yet again. 'But let's hope they'll
remember what you said when it's dumping time. Will
we be busy this afternoon, do you think?'

'There were three admissions over the weekend; two
men and an old lady with a badly fractured shaft of
humerus—just for a change.'

'And she was admitted?'

'Yes, she's another like Miss Marshall, living alone
in a top flat, and the convalescent ward is full. If the
MSW can't find her suitable temporary accommo-
dation, Mr Wilkie will have to cancel his hip replacement scheduled for Wednesday.'

They had now arrived, and the central corridor of
the unit was buzzing. 'That must have been some
emergency,' deduced Sonia, eyeing all the activity.
'Looks like lover boy's in for a busy afternoon.'

Marnie was surprised to find herself resenting that
slighting reference to James. She bit back an angry
retort and said instead, quite mildly, 'At least it'll keep

him out of my hair. Give me a shout when you're ready to get Basher up.' Then, with a careless wave of the hand, she peeled off into the women's ward.

At first glance, all looked peaceful, with patients dozing over magazines with their glasses at half-mast, or avidly watching a film on television in the day-room. But Jinty and Judy made sure that Marnie didn't relax by giving her half an hour of subtle teasing. Marnie was glad when Sister came bustling up to tell her all about Mrs Tweedie, the new patient. 'And young Peggy Aird is ready for crutches whenever you've got a minute,' Sister remembered, as she bustled off again.

Marnie went to Mrs Tweedie first. Her whole arm was a swollen and discoloured mass of bruising, despite her fracture being above the elbow. She pulled up a chair and introduced herself before asking her patient to try and move her fingers.

The response was a barely perceptible twiddle. 'And I can't lift ma wrist, Nurse,' Mrs Tweedie complained. 'It feels as if it wasna there.'

Marnie had been afraid of that. Patients who escaped without damage to the radial nerve in such circumstances were the lucky ones. When she went to fetch crutches for Peggy, Marnie left a note on Sister's desk in case she'd been the first to spot Mrs Tweedie's paralysis. She had to pass the men's ward, where nurses and porters were lifting an unconscious figure on to a bed. Two more beds awaited other casualties. James was indeed having a busy afternoon.

So busy, in fact, that he was still in Theatre when Marnie and Sonia returned to Physio, comparing notes as they went. Andrew Wilkie would be doing his weekly ward-round next day and Sonia needed full reports.

On her desk, Marnie found several notes, all relating

to calls made during her absence. The unit administrator was querying last month's figures, but he would
be halfway home now. The laundry manager, ditto.
The professor of geriatrics wanted to talk about
increased physio time for his new daycare centre opening next week. Marnie snorted with disgust. Lucky for
him she'd foreseen this necessity ages ago and had put
in a strongly worded request for another member of
staff. Of course, asking was one thing and getting quite
another, she reflected, as she set off to tell him all that
as tactfully as possible.

She got his stock response for dealing with all female
staff; a mixture of condescension and bedside manner.
The meeting left her feeling both angry and frustrated,
and she was frowning heavily as she passed a small
group of green-capped and gowned figures outside
Theatre on her way back to base.

'Looks as if your girlfriend has had a bad day,
James,' observed the senior anaesthetist humorously.

James promptly swung round and reached out to
grab Marnie's arm and ask, 'What's the matter,
sweetheart?'

'I've just been patronised by a member of your
profession who ought to know better,' she returned
sadly.

'Tell me who it was and I'll fight him at dawn,'
offered James, getting hearty guffaws of appreciation
from his colleagues.

Marnie faced the lot of them with a beautiful smile
she was far from feeling. 'I'm glad to note that chauvin-
ism continues to flourish within these hallowed walls,'
she said sweetly. 'It makes my job so much more—
interesting.'

More appreciative laughter, for her this time.

'You've met your match at last, James,' considered the senior anaesthetist, as James walked on with Marnie.

'I know that—and I'm absolutely terrified,' James called back, looking anything but. He bent down to Marnie, asking, 'Who was it who upset you?'

'Professor Matthew. Who else?'

'Darling, he upsets everybody—male and female— so there was nothing personal in it.'

'He just wouldn't listen when I tried to tell him he can't expect me to conjure extra physios out of thin air. Just patted my shoulder and told me he knew he could count on me.' *Why am I telling him my troubles?* Marnie asked herself. *Why?*

James put an arm around her waist and squeezed her for a second, treating her to a strong whiff of antiseptic as well as a rapid rise in pulse-rate. 'I had a run-in with him myself only last week, about his idea for an acute ortho-geriatric ward. Very good in itself, but not exactly for instant achievement—and, except for the pat on the shoulder, his response was identical. The man is just wildly impractical. Are you finished for the day, Marnie?' James finished.

'I hope so.'

'Then how about something to eat at the Waterman around the corner as soon as I've changed? I'm sorry it has to be on the doorstep, but I'm on tonight and I want to be near the afternoon admissions.'

'They're serious, then?' queried Marnie.

'Two are. A badly fractured pelvis with some bladder damage and a young lad with an arm that was practically ripped off. I've sewn it back on, but——' James broke off abruptly, hitting himself quite hard on the side of the head. 'Shut up, you insensitive fool! You'll put the poor girl off her supper. Did you get lunch, Marnie?'

'Yes, thanks. I raided your carrier bag.'

'Good girl! You must eat regularly, you know, no matter how busy you may be,' said James, sounding for all the world like an anxious nanny.

There's so much niceness in him, thought Marnie, as they reached her department. 'What about your own lunch, though, James?' she asked.

'Oh, Theatre Sister got me a sandwich in between ops,' he returned airily. 'She's a very good pal of mine.'

'You've got a lot of those,' retorted Marnie with an abrupt change of feeling.

'Good pals? Yes, I believe I have. I'm very lucky.' James bent down to plant a kiss on the tip of her neat little nose. 'Back in ten minutes, love, so don't linger.' And off he went, arms swinging and rubber boots squeaking vigorously on the vinyl-covered corridor.

Marnie was glad he had mentioned Sister Helen Ballantyne, who was generally supposed to adore him. She'd been in serious danger of beginning to like him, and that could be very dangerous when he attracted her so much. Having been more or less bounced into this piece of play-acting, Marnie intended to come out of it unscathed.

'I don't like you in blue,' James said candidly when he returned, dressed himself in trousers and an open-necked shirt. 'It makes you look cool and unreachable.'

'Good,' said Marnie, smoothing down her neat shirt-waister. 'Because that's exactly what I am—to you.'

'You weren't on Saturday night,' he reminded her softly.

Marnie flushed at the memory. 'On Saturday night I was—disarmed by drink.'

'One gin and tonic and a couple of glasses of burgundy,' he remembered. 'So it doesn't take very much to melt the ice-maiden.'

'My melting point is quite irrelevant,' she insisted firmly. 'This is just an act we're putting on for others, remember?'

'I'll try,' he promised, 'but it's going to be damn difficult.'

'Not if I help by always wearing blue,' she said. 'Shall we go out through the side gate? It's quicker.'

'True, but not sufficiently conspicuous,' James returned, seizing her elbow and steering her towards the main exit, where their departure was observed by two consultants, the hall porter and a student nurse. 'Not too bad for a start,' he said, 'and with luck, the Waterman will be packed with familiar faces.'

'Now listen, James, tonight's meal is on me,' said Marnie resolutely as he held open the pub door for her.

He laughed at her. 'Oh, very sensible! Let them all see you paying and they'll think I'm your latest toy boy.'

'In view of our relative ages, I doubt that,' Marnie returned, trying hard not to laugh and not quite succeeding. 'Anyway, I'm not that daft. I shall give you the money afterwards, when we're alone.'

'I can think of much better things than that to do when we're alone,' he whispered in her ear as they entered the lounge bar.

Luck was with them. Two housemen were sitting with two young nurses. 'Bringing the number of spotters to eight so far tonight,' remarked James with obvious satisfaction. 'This was a brilliant idea of mine.'

'So brilliant that we can probably call this off sooner than we thought?' suggested Marnie as they raced another couple to a vacant corner table.

James waited until they were seated before answering. 'If a thing's worth doing, it's worth doing well,' he intoned piously. 'Hot or cold?'

'I beg your pardon?'

'Do you fancy a salad or something cooked?'

'I'd like chilli con carne,' decided Marnie without looking at the menu.

James noticed that. 'So you often come here, then,' he assumed when he had given their order.

'Now and again—usually when I'm on call.'

'I didn't think heads of department were required to do on call.'

'We're not, but I often do when we are really pushed—like now, with Lynne and Betty and Fiona——' Marnie stopped. For the moment, she'd quite forgotten his involvement with Fiona.

James looked startled. 'She's not still missing, is she?'

'No, she's been on holiday. I expect her back tomorrow.'

'That's all right, then. As I said, she's a nice wee thing, but rather impressionable.'

'And you, James, are the one who made the impression.'

James frowned and scratched his ear. 'I know—but who'd have thought it? I'm damn nearly old enough to be her father.'

'In that case, why did you take her out?' she asked reasonably.

'I didn't. Well, not in that way.'

Marnie cupped her chin in her hands and planted her elbows on the table. 'Do tell—I'm fascinated,' she said ironically.

'Fiona's mother is related in some way to my eldest sister's husband, and when Fiona came to Duntrune hot on the heels of the latest boyfriend, Nan—her mother—asked Clare and John to keep an eye on her. It seems the lad's not approved of, so——'

'That doesn't explain why——'

'Let me finish, will you? Clare had her out to the house one weekend a while back when I was there, so I got the job of running the child home.' James paused, looking rueful. 'My big mistake was taking her to the sailing club regatta, but when Helen Ballantyne stood me up at the last minute I didn't fancy going alone. There's a girl there who—but that's another story. Anyway, the child claims to be mad about boats, and I just thought she might enjoy it. Marnie, are you listening?'

'Yes, of course, James. You thought Fiona would enjoy the regatta. . .' Yes, she had been listening, but also she'd been very intrigued to hear that Helen Ballantyne, the supposedly adoring theatre sister, had stood him up.

'Yes, well, after that Fiona seemed to think we were practically engaged, which was no end of a bore, I can tell you. I had a devil of a job detaching her.'

'Did you make love to her?' Marnie asked bluntly.

James scowled blackly. 'For God's sake, Marnie, what do you take me for?'

'I only asked because if you did it would explain her—misreading of the situation.'

'Possibly—but I didn't. Unless you count an avuncular peck on the cheek?'

'Of course not—but as you say, Fiona's very impressionable.'

'Hearing about us should complete the cure, though,' said James thoughtfully, as the waitress brought their food.

'That thought has occurred to me too,' Marnie told him. 'And I can't decide how to deal with it.'

'Do you have to? Surely the problem is hers. If wee girls go weaving fantasies, then they must expect to get hurt when they come up against reality.'

Reality? Where was the reality in their relationship? 'You're very—practical, James,' remarked Marnie.

'If you really mean heartless, then why not say so?'

'D'you know, we could easily turn this argument into the final fatal quarrel if you like,' she realised.

James surprised her then as he had so often during the last few days. He stretched out and seized her wrists, pinning them down on the table. 'I'm glad you said that,' he insisted. 'I was in danger of forgetting this is supposed to be a game. Three or four weeks, I said——' he'd said two, maximum '—and that's what it'll take. At least. But I'm very glad we've cleared the air about Fiona. You thought I'd seduced her!'

Marnie blinked. 'Well, I——'

'For your information, little ingénues straight out of college are not my type.'

'So who is?' asked Marnie, thinking of all the girls James had managed to get through.

He released her wrists and sat back, regarding her thoughtfully for several seconds. 'Now that,' he said, 'would be telling.' Then he picked up his knife and fork and started on his steak.

Marnie watched him as he ate. He was without question the most attractive man she had ever known. Even more so now than when, as a harum-scarum medical student, he had been the boy next door but three on whom she'd had her first crush. Lines of thought and concentration were beginning to appear round his eyes, a hint of grey in his thick black curly hair, an almost imperceptible blurring of the jaw-line. . . She turned her attention to his hands, brown and strong, the nails cut short as befitted a surgeon.

Hands that could perform miracles of repair and reconstruction. And send shivers of delight coursing through foolish females. . . Marnie drew a quick breath, snatching up her fork and thrusting it into her food.

James looked up. 'Too hot for you, sweetie?' he asked solicitously, laying down his knife to pour her some iced water.

'No—yes. . .thank you. You're very kind.'

'I know,' he said, 'and I'm so glad it's finally dawned on you.'

'Why?' she felt driven to ask.

'Because I'd rather be appreciated than disapproved of.'

Well, what had she expected him to say? 'Who wouldn't?' she asked, smiling brightly to hide her confusion.

James met that with a broad grin. 'How about our revered Professor Matthew for one? Or could it be that he's much too self-absorbed to notice the difference?'

Marnie chuckled, James did too, and they were laughing into each other's eyes when the four young doctors and nurses left unnoticed by either of them. Fresh fuel for the latest hospital bonfire tomorrow.

When the waitress came to remove their plates and ask about dessert, James asked Marnie if she'd mind settling for coffee only as he was rather anxious to get back and take another look at his afternoon emergencies.

'Of course not,' she agreed readily. 'Anyway, I have to be making a move myself.' She didn't add that that was because she was meeting Dominic for a drink.

'But you shall have the full treatment tomorrow,' promised James. 'You are free tomorrow?'

'I—could be,' said Marnie, determined not to sound too eager.

James frowned. 'Don't strain yourself. After all, this is only for your sake.'

'Oh, dear, did I sound ungrateful? I didn't mean to. Sorry.'

'And so you should be. Now then, just in case we don't get a chance to talk tomorrow, I'll pick you up at your place at seven.'

'Right. And will I try to arrange to be chatting on the landing with the Wilkies when you arrive?'

'You're catching on,' said James approvingly, stretching out to squeeze her hand.

They drank their coffee, exchanged hospital talk as they returned and parted in the car park with nothing more intimate than another squeezing of hands, among all the visitors. But the look in his eyes was a caress.

When he had gone striding away, Marnie now probably forgotten in his eagerness to get back to work, she sat in her car for quite a while before driving off to meet Dominic. However confidently she might begin a session with James, he invariably left her feeling confused and vulnerable.

Over the years, she had built up a picture of him in her mind and taken up a standpoint of disapproval. He was a fine surgeon, trusted and admired by patients and colleagues alike. He was also—not to mince words—a philanderer whom women trusted at their peril. Two weeks ago she had accepted Fiona's story without question. Now James had given her his version, which rang equally true. Whom to believe?

Marnie shifted restlessly in her seat. Yet did it matter? James was playing this game for some obscure reason of his own—she'd come round to Sonia's way of thinking—and, one day in the not too distant future, he'd get tired of it. Watch out for the signs, Marnie, and make sure you're the one to walk away first. That's the only thing you can do, she told herself.

Coming to such a sensible conclusion should have left her feeling more satisfied than this. With an exclamation of impatience, Marnie switched on the ignition and took off fast, away from trouble and towards an hour or two of calm in Dominic's undisturbing presence.

At the bus stop just beyond the gates, two young nurses were waiting. Reminded of her own experience the week before, Marnie stopped to offer them a lift, which was gratefully accepted when she said she was headed for town.

Yes, Bank Street would be fine, they said, and by good luck there was a parking bay free right behind Dominic's white Mercedes—another step up the ladder, and it would be a Porsche.

Marnie said goodnight to the girls and locked her car, just as Dominic came to meet her.

CHAPTER SIX

'COME what may, I'm going to get to the hairdresser's by five today,' Marnie told Sonia next morning.

'Oh, yes—got a date, have we?' asked Sonia.

'Yesterday, you were worried in case I hadn't.'

'I hope you know what you're doing, Marnie.'

Marnie opened her violet eyes very wide. 'I thought we'd settled all that. I'm teaching James the Lad a lesson, am I not?' Twelve hours of non-exposure to the man had quite restored her poise and confidence.

'Well, if anybody can do that, I believe you can,' said Sonia.

'Thanks, Sonia, I appreciate that. Now wish me equal luck in dealing with our two truants, Fiona and Betty.'

'As if you needed it—a wizard like you at staff relations. See you later.'

When Belle asked which of the truants Marnie wished to interview first, Marnie opted for Betty. She began by hoping that Betty was feeling better, Betty said she was, whereupon Marnie put on a serious look and said it was time to get to the bottom of Betty's trouble, so how about asking her GP to refer her to the hospital's leading consultant on internal medicine? Betty winced and hummed and haaed, after which Marnie left her in no doubt about her choices. No more self-donated long weekends—or a medical consultation. Betty went out, suitably chastened. If only dealing with Fiona could be as straightforward!

Fiona came in looking white and defiant, eyeing her boss with a malevolence that told she'd already been brought up to date on the latest hospital sensation.

Marnie decided not to notice. 'I hope you're feeling the better for your holiday, Fiona,' she began.

'A bit.'

'Miss Craig is very happy to have you transfer to the Western, if you're still wanting to leave here.'

'Wouldn't you?'

Marnie thought that could be a distinct possibility, and very soon too, if opinion was divided on who ditched whom! Only she wouldn't have the choice. 'One can't go through life running away from every disappointment, Fiona.'

'What would you know about it?'

'Never in my life have I run from a problem,' Marnie returned as patiently as she could manage. 'But it's your career we're discussing, not mine. Shall I tell Miss Craig to expect you after your twenty-eight days' notice is up, then?'

'You may as well, I s'pose. There's nothing for me here now.' Her glare told Marnie whom she was holding responsible for that.

'Very well—and for the next few days I'd like you to assist on the intensive care unit. Mrs Carter is snowed under at the moment.'

Fiona's eyes brightened. She'd been angling to get on to ICU ever since she came. 'Thanks for the consolation prize,' she said sarcastically, going out and banging the door.

Marnie slumped in her chair, cursing the tender conscience that had prompted that gesture. It would have made much more sense to send Betty to Ortho, give Fiona Betty's list and help out on ICU herself.

Now she'd have to go on helping Sonia for another week, inviting yet more exposure to James and the hospital gossips. 'I'm nuts!' sighed Marnie as she reached for the 'In' tray.

Despite her numerous admin duties, she made it up to Ortho by ten-thirty. 'I've been meaning to ask for days—what about your outpatients?' Sonia said belatedly.

'I've managed to squeeze them all in between one and half-past three, which they quite like.' And James will not!

'What about your own lunch?'

'Who needs an hour to eat a sandwich?' asked Marnie robustly. 'Now, then, what's new?'

'Mrs Nairn to pre-op for her hip replacement tomorrow, and Mrs Ferguson can get up today.'

'Fine. Now are you sure you can manage all the men?'

Sonia insisted that she could, if Marnie would continue to treat the women.

She's trying to spare me all the cheek and innuendo, realised Marnie gratefully. It was too much to hope that the men didn't know all about her and James.

The houseman was with Mrs Nairn, giving her her admission once-over, so Marnie began with Peggy Aird. 'Right! Stairs today,' she said.

'What? On one leg and a crutch? I'd rather go up and down on ma backside!' protested Peggy.

'Don't forget you've got the banister rail too, so it's easier than you think. Here, I'll show you.' Which was how Marnie happened to be hopping downstairs as James came bounding up.

'You do like to get inside a part, do you not?' he teased when they met on the half landing. 'So I'm really looking forward to tonight.'

Marnie ignored that last bit. 'Peggy was doubtful, so I decided to give her a demonstration. Mr Dalgleish,' she added for the ears of Peggy, alert and watchful.

His lips twitched in acknowledgement. 'Quite right, Miss Fraser-Firth. Never ask a patient to try anything you're not prepared to try on yourself. Unless of course you're a surgeon,' he added *sotto voce*.

Marnie giggled and James purred, 'Darling, you're so enchanting when you laugh,' before sweeping on to exchange a few words with Peggy Aird. He never passed any of his patients without that.

'He's so marvellous,' breathed Peggy, who was still gazing after him when Marnie rejoined her. 'You *are* lucky, miss!'

'Yes, Mr Dalgleish is certainly a pleasure to work with,' returned Marnie, daring Peggy to comment further.

'And I bet he's even more of a pleasure to play with,' returned the girl saucily.

To that, Marnie could only say weakly that it was high time they got down to some work.

Mrs Ferguson was overjoyed to be mobile. Nosy by nature, she had missed far too much of the comings and goings until now. Mrs Kerr didn't think she'd bother today, thank you, dear, if it was all the same to Marnie. Marnie said that no, it wasn't, and a gentle argument ensued until Mrs Kerr decided she needed to go to the bathroom. As this meant quite a long walk, honour was more or less satisfied on both sides—for the moment.

By then the houseman had finished examining Mrs Nairn. She was dreading her coming operation and had only agreed to it because she was now too lame to manage her invalid mother. Marnie spent a long time painting a picture of a procedure which was now almost as commonplace as having the appendix out. To this Mrs Nairn replied that her great-uncle by marriage had died after having his appendix out in 1917.

Marnie took a deep breath and said things had improved a lot since then, before asking Mrs Leuchars, who had had both hips replaced and was in now to get her bunions sorted, if she'd mind parading up and down for the new patient's benefit. 'See me, I'd rather get ma hips done than a tooth filled,' claimed Mrs Leuchars, doing more good in one minute than Marnie had in ten.

I should have thought of that sooner, realised Marnie, getting down to business at last. 'Just some hip measurements, and a look at your muscles,' she said. 'We'll need to do some building up here, I see. A limp does so throw a body out of kilter. Now for the basic drill you'll need to keep up for a few weeks afterwards. . .'

The office phone was ringing when Marnie got back to base at lunchtime. Surely somebody could have answered? she thought, running the last few yards, only to be glad that nobody had bothered when she picked it up and heard James's deep voice. 'Sorry, Marnie, but I can't make lunch today. Emergency.'

'That's all right, James. I wasn't expecting you.' Well done, girl, you're improving! 'I'm sorry you're so busy, though.'

He ignored that. 'If you weren't expecting me, then you should have been. I said I was coming.' He sounded quite cross.

Marnie wondered why. 'I'm sorry—I must have forgotten.'

'Thank you, I'm very flattered,' he said drily, 'but then such a lot of interesting things have happened since we met last.'

What on earth had got into him? 'I think you must be tired,' she decided in a soothing voice. 'If you'd rather cry off tonight, I'll quite understand.'

'How very kind of you, but that'll not be necessary—though I could be a bit late.'

'That's all right,' she repeated, 'and if you *do* change your mind——'

'I shan't,' he said brusquely. 'And I should make it by half-past at the latest. Now I have to go.' Click, and the phone went dead. Marnie looked at it as if it ought to explain why James had sounded so cross, just because she wanted to make it easy for him to break their date, if he wanted to. Correction, not their date. It wasn't a date. It was the next phase in the face-saving campaign. Was he sick of it already? He'd seemed keen enough last night. . . No time to puzle that out now, though, if she was to grab a bite to eat before the first patients arrived.

Marnie only had eight now—she hadn't dared take on any more while the staffing situation was so erratic—and, as she specialised in manipulation, it was no surprise that most of them had back problems. All were improving, except Mrs McAndrew.

'You've been lifting heavy boxes again,' Marnie guessed. Mrs McAndrew helped her husband in his corner shop.

'No, dear, not since you told me not to.' A pause. 'Now I sort of push 'em along the floor, with ma knee.'

'Does that not hurt your back too?'

'Aye—a bit. But not so much as lifting.'

'No lifting, humping, pushing or otherwise shifting heavy weights in any way whatsoever until you're pain-free and I'm satisfied with your check X-ray, Mrs McAndrew,' ordained Marnie, wishing she'd been that specific before. But then how many patients were that ingenious?

'Rab'll not like that,' said the patient.

'Surely Rab'd like it even less if you did yourself a permanent injury and couldn't help him at all?' said Marnie. 'I think I'd better give you a note to take home, so he'll know you're not just skiving.'

'The way some men treat their wives is enough to put a girl right off matrimony altogether,' said Marnie to Sonia when she rejoined her on the wards some time later.

'I thought you were off it already,' returned her friend.

Marnie ignored that. 'I was thinking of one of my patients. What do you think of this?' She relayed her chat with Mrs McAndrew and Sonia agreed, before asking with apparent irrelevance how Marnie really felt about Dominic.

Marnie was surprised, but she answered, 'We're very good friends who enjoy the same things. I thought you knew that.'

'And you're not afraid that your present little—er—caper with James the Lad might sour the relationship?'

'Why on earth should it? Besides, how is Dominic to find out, unless somebody tells him? And I'm not going to.'

'No, of course not; silly of me.' Sonia changed tack. 'Do you feel strong enough to help me with Basher now? That boy gets worse every day. . .' They were soon away on a discussion of all the likely reasons, and the chance of any complications in Marnie's personal life was forgotten.

At a quarter to eight, and in spite of deciding not to only minutes before, Marnie went out on to her little terrace again, to look down into the car park for a sight of James's car. She'd made it to the hairdresser with seconds to spare and then got home in nice time to enjoy a cool, relaxing bath before putting on a dress of pale lavender silk that went well with her eyes. James hadn't told her where they were going, but he had promised her the full treatment, so she'd supposed it was somewhere fairly grand and had dressed accordingly. Now it was looking rather as though the bastard had stood her up. He *is* about to dump me, she thought with something approaching panic, when the sound of a car prompted another look. She saw a black car glide to a halt and then James getting out.

Marnie waited until he buzzed and announced himself before pressing the door release button. It would never do to let him know she'd been keeping watch!

He must have taken the stairs two at a time, because she'd hardly turned away before the doorbell rang. She opened the door with a smile of just the right temperature, to find Susan Wilkie on the doorstep, looking hot and bothered, and wearing an apron over her dress. 'Oh, Marnie, can you save my life?' she begged. 'I'm doing Andrew his favourite pudding, and the cream's gone off.'

'I've only got some Long-Life, but come in while I get it,' beamed Marnie, thinking how fortuitous this was, with James on his way up.

A second later they were all three in the hall. 'Why, James,' fluttered Susan, 'fancy seeing you.'

'It is my night off,' he answered with a smile, before leaning down to kiss Marnie lingeringly on the lips. 'So sorry I'm late, darling, but you know how it is. That clinic just went on and on! Never mind—I'm here now, safe and sound.'

Just as though she were the anxious little woman,

awaiting her man's return. He never missed a trick. 'So I see,' said Marnie. 'Are you sure there's nothing else you need, Susan?'

'No, thanks, dear—just the cream. Well, have a lovely time, you two,' and Susan scurried off to tell Andrew that James was there—again! And the two of them just so star-struck. . .

'I'd begun to think you weren't coming,' Marnie said as she locked the door.

'Would you rather I hadn't?' James asked bluntly.

'What? After I went to all this trouble?'

Soberly, he looked her up and down. 'I have to say it was well worth it. And you're not wearing blue. I find that quite—encouraging.'

'I could always go back in and change,' she offered.

'Certainly not! We're late enough as it is.' He took her arm and hustled her down the stairs.

'Where are we going?' asked Marnie, who was having difficulty keeping up with him.

'Lednoch House.'

Madly expensive and nearly twenty miles away. 'Will there be anybody from the hospital there to see us?' she queried.

After the faintest hesitation James said, 'If my intelligence is reliable.'

'Only it's rather far out, so I thought——'

'We could try somewhere in town if you'd rather. The Blue Crocodile, perhaps.'

The place where she had been with Dominic the night before, and where he'd probably be eating tonight!

'No, thanks,' she returned hurriedly.

'You sound rather guilty,' he remarked as he opened the car door for her. 'I wonder why?'

Marnie suddenly remembered that the two young

nurses she had given a lift to last night were on Theatre. When James got in beside her, she said, 'You know, don't you? You knew at lunchtime. That's why you sounded so cross.'

'Of course I was cross,' he said. 'There was I beavering away to save your face, and you sabotaged my efforts. It would have served you right if I hadn't turned up tonight.'

'So why did you?' she asked.

'Because I'm exceptionally goodnatured,' he insisted. And then, 'I wonder if your crocodile friend would be quite so generous if he got to hear we spent the night together last week?'

'How would he? And anyway, we didn't!'

'I think we've already shown how easily folk can be fooled,' he pointed out.

'Are you threatening me?' demanded Marnie.

'Don't be silly! How can I upset things when I know nothing about him—except that he looks like an under-nourished clerk and drives a flashy car to make up for it? That's rather a pity. Nobody's going to believe you ditched me for him.'

'God, but you're conceited!' flashed Marnie.

'You've said that before,' he retorted.

'Well, you are. You're the most—the most. . .'

'The sooner I get a gin and tonic and a couple of glasses of burgundy into you, the better,' considered James as they hit the motorway and headed west.

'Have you been here before?' asked James as he swung the car in at the entrance to the hotel drive.

'Only once—when my father was entertaining some overseas surgeons.'

'And now you're about to entertain a home-grown

one. Smile nicely, now. I've been looking forward to this.'

So had Marnie, if truth be told, but she wasn't going to say so. 'I'll play my part,' she said. 'I know you only want to help me.'

James handed her out of the car and kept hold of her hand, standing close and looking down at her with narrowed eyes. 'Why is it that I trust you least when you seem most compliant?' he wondered.

Marnie stood up to that well, considering her knees were trembling. 'Is it my fault you've got a suspicious nature?' she asked with wonderful simplicity.

His hand tightened on hers. 'There's one thing I blame you for, but it's not that,' he returned enigmatically. 'And don't ask me what it is, because I'm not going to tell you.'

'Right then—shan't!' returned Marnie in a childish treble and with a pettish shrug that had him laughing and ruffling her curls as they walked towards the entrance.

At first, Marnie thought he'd slipped up when, gin and tonic in hand, she looked round the bar and failed to see anybody from the hospital. Later, though, in the vaulted dining-room, she spotted the unit general manager with his wife. Except that she didn't recognise the lady.

Neither did James. 'This is going to be more fun than I thought,' he exulted, stopping dead and leaving the head waiter to carry on alone. He took Marnie on a detour that took them past the admin man's table, where he did a very good job of spoiling Mr Cooper's evening, before leading away a Marnie who was shaking with suppressed laughter. 'Remind me to look in the register on the way out,' he said, when the head waiter had settled them at their table. 'We must find out if Mr and Mrs MacSmith are staying the night.'

'Stop, unless you want me to explode,' implored Marnie, wiping her streaming eyes. 'Anyway, what if they are? They're only committing the indiscretion we're supposed to have indulged in.' She sobered down. 'The plan has misfired,' she said. 'He'll never confess to seeing us here.'

James was indignant on two counts. 'You're forgetting something. We're free agents, and he's a married man.'

Marnie gazed at him, eyes wide. 'Somehow I never saw you as an upholder of holy matrimony,' she remarked.

He ignored that dig. 'And we haven't come all this way for nothing either. If that's an innocent little dinner party, then why should he not mention seeing us? And if it isn't——' his eyes took on their wicked gleam '—we'll collect some sheets of headed writing paper from the lounge after dinner.'

'What on earth for?' Marnie queried.

'Just the thing on which to present our next requests for more funds.'

Marnie threw back her head and laughed aloud. 'James, you're absolutely priceless! I can almost believe you would do that.'

'I might,' he said, 'but do go on. I'm enjoying this.'

But she had simmered down again. 'You didn't really know they were coming tonight, did you? I mean—how could you?'

'No, I didn't,' he admitted.

'Then why——?'

'Because this is where I wanted to bring you.'

'Why?' she asked again.

'Perhaps I wanted to impress you. Perhaps I thought

you were worth it,' he added so softly that she almost didn't hear in the subdued buzz of conversation all around.

'I don't know what to say,' she said in an excited whisper.

'That makes a nice change,' James considered as the waiters brought their first course and a bottle of burgundy for inspection. James looked at the label and nodded.

'Does red burgundy really go with medallions of pork?' wondered Marnie.

'Just about. If you're not too fussy.'

'My father usually chooses a white.'

'Fine, but his priorities will be different from mine.'

'I'm not sure I get your point,' she said.

'Never mind. Isn't this smoked salmon good?'

'The best I've ever tasted. Oh, James. . .'

'Yes, Marnie?'

'I'm having such a lovely time.'

The warm intimacy of his answering smile sent her quite dizzy. 'Three cheers for the genius who invented gin,' he said.

Marnie giggled like a schoolgirl. 'Oh, James, what an extraordinary thing to say!'

By the time the waiter brought their coffee, Marnie had quite forgotten why she was here with a man of whom she'd always made a point of disapproving. There was no past and no future; only the here and now in this lovely room with this lovely food and wine and that wonderfully, kind, amusing and attractive man sitting across the table from her, infusing her with his zest for life; making her feel more vital and attractive than ever before.

James watched the transformation, a tiny smile of satisfaction playing about his mouth as he led her into more and more absurdities with a well-placed word or two, and regular, unobserved toppings up of her wine glass.

'I am very much afraid I'm just the littlest bit tipsy,' confided Marnie when it was time to leave and she caught her foot against the table leg.

'Then take my arm, sweetheart,' invited James. 'After all, what are friends for?'

'And you're—such a very good friend, James.'

'No more than you deserve, dear,' he insisted, steering her expertly out of the room.

Watching him pay the bill at the reception desk brought back some hazy memories for Marnie. 'My Crocodile friend and I always go Dutch,' she said, fumbling in her bag for her purse, once they were in the car.

James's eyebrows rose steeply. 'The devil you do!' he exclaimed. 'I dislike the sound of that guy more and more with each thing I hear about him.'

'Except when he's feeling amorous,' Marnie remembered. 'Then he pays for me as well.'

'I don't believe what I'm hearing,' said James, sounding as if he didn't like it either. 'That's disgusting!'

'Why?' asked tipsy Marnie serenely. 'It's not as if he does much—hardly anything, really. Just a kiss and a bit of a cuddle. And he's not very good at that.'

'I'm absolutely speechless!' foamed James, going on to prove the opposite. 'How come a wonderful, special girl like you can put up with such a tight-fisted, incompetent fool? Let alone get started with him in the first place! What's the attraction?'

Marnie swayed round in her seat and held up a wobbly forefinger. 'I shall explain,' she said. 'It is extremely handy to have a man to go about with—to concerts and things. Especially when all your girl

friends are married or co-hab—co-hab. . .otherwise
fixed up.'

'Handier than having a sex life?' he enquired.

'Oh, sex,' said Marnie, dismissing it with another
wave of that finger. 'I'm pretty sure I could only get
really interested in sex if I was madly in love. And
then——' She whistled loud and long to show him how
much. 'Only I never have been—I can't think why. But
it's rather a drawback in the present free-for-all.'

'I can see it must be,' said James faintly. And then
in a firmer voice, 'Are you honestly saying you've
never been to bed with a man?'

'No, I'm not actually saying that,' she answered,
remembering inexpert teenage fumblings and that curi-
ous, passionless weekend with Dominic. 'Just that I
think it's very overrated.'

'Unless you happen to be in love,' prompted James.
He seemed very anxious to get his facts right.

'Yes. But don't let me put you off. That's only my
view. Most women would probably not agree. And as
for men——' Marnie whistled again. 'Except, of
course, for Dominic. Do you know, sometimes I
wonder if he——'

'I'm not feeling quite strong enough to continue this
conversation,' said James, leaning over to make sure
her seat belt was properly fastened. Then he switched
on the ignition and backed out.

'I'm very much afraid that I may have shocked you,'
said Marnie politely.

'Shocked me? No. Astounded me, more like. I'd no
idea the world was quite so full of idiotic and incompetent males.'

'But I'm sure you're neither, James,' she assured
him earnestly.

'When I'm with you, I'm all too inclined to feel both,' he answered with a sigh of bewilderment.

By the time they reached Duntrune, Marnie was asleep, her head drooping sideways on to his shoulder. The journey had taken twice as long as the outward one, because James had taken the greatest care so as not to disturb her. When they got to the flats she was still drowsy and unsteady on her feet. Seems I overdid the anti-freeze tonight,' muttered James. 'Here, give me that key, darling. You've got it upside down.'

Once inside, he scooped her up in his arms, carried her to the lift, and then into her flat, with Marnie making no protest whatever. Having seen her safely into an armchair, James went in search of her bedroom. Having located it, he came back and pulled her to her feet. 'Come on, sweetie, you can't spend the night here,' he said gently. 'Nor in that gorgeous dress either.' He sighed. 'Ah well, in for a penny. . .' He unzipped it and let it drop to the floor.

When he had laid her on the bed and pulled up the duvet, she said, 'Thank you, but I have to brush my teeth, and so on.'

James smiled crookedly. 'Thank heaven you're not as far gone as I'd feared. Are you sure you can manage?'

Marnie giggled. 'What will you do if I can't? she asked. But she was more alert now.

'You'll cope,' he said, 'so I'll be off. And Marnie, I'm very, very sorry.'

She sat on the side of the bed and looked at him. 'What for?' she asked.

'Getting you drunk.'

'I am not drunk,' she articulated with great dignity. 'I am merely a trifle in—out—incommoded.' And with a tiny hiccup, she wove her way into the en-suite and shut the door.

CHAPTER SEVEN

MARNIE awoke next morning with a dry mouth and a throbbing head. When she raised it from the pillow to look at the clock, the room went round. She lay down again and tried to think.

Last night, James had taken her out to dinner. The meal had been wonderful and so had he, but she must have drunk a lot more than was good for her, because she had this uncomfortable feeling that she'd talked rather a lot about Dominic. Why? Had she been trying to make James jealous? What a hope! And what exactly had she said? She'd give a lot to remember that.

A cold shower, four Disprins and a couple of black coffees later, Marnie was sitting at the kitchen table with her head in her hands; not because it was throbbing, although it was, but because she was remembering rather more. What had possessed her to talk about Dominic at all? Let alone go into details of their sex life—or lack of it. She had so wanted James to see her as sophisticated, experienced and aware. Now he must think she was some kind of nutter! She dreaded their next meeting. How embarrassing it would be. Abandon those silly hopes you were beginning to have about him, Marnie, she told herself. All you can hope for now is that he'll keep to his promise about letting you dump him. The sooner the better. And if that isn't soon enough to still the wagging tongues, then too bad.

'Super, actually,' said Marnie lightly when Sonia asked her how the previous evening had gone. 'We went to

Lednoch House, no less—and caught our revered general manager dining with a lady not his wife!'

'Fancy that,' said Sonia, who had another, more important question. 'Did James make love to you?'

'He never laid a finger on me,' claimed Marnie. And neither he had, in the way that Sonia meant. 'He behaved like a perfect gentleman all evening.'

'If that's true, then he's either in love with you or he's sickening for something,' considered Marnie's best friend. 'When are you seeing him again?'

Marnie dodged that by saying she'd been thinking over what Sonia had said about spoiling her relationship with Dominic, that Sonia was quite right and it wasn't worth risking. So all in all, she'd decided it was time to call a halt.

'And what does lover boy think of that?' asked Sonia.

'James? I haven't told him yet, but I'm sure he'll understand. I could be wrong, but I suspect he's finding saving my face rather tedious.'

'Perhaps he is and perhaps he's not. What I'd really like to know is just why he started all this in the first place.'

Marnie had explained once and didn't feel up to doing so again. Especially now that it was all over. She changed the subject by flourishing a letter she'd been reading when Sonia came in. 'Talk about muddle,' she said. 'Here's the finance department wanting our yearly forecast for tomorrow's meeting instead of next month's, so I'm afraid that'll have to be my priority this morning. It has to be in by lunchtime.'

'That's all right,' said Sonia easily. 'Andrew Wilkie's ops cases'll not need treating, and with so many going off to the convalescent hospital it should be a fairly quiet day. So good luck with the figures. Why not tell

them all our electrical stuff's gone critical and we need
a quarter of a million?' And with that interesting idea,
Sonia eventually took herself off.

Marnie agreed to the complicated swapping of evening duties which three of her junior staff requested,
and then dealt with a few other outstanding queries
before settling down to forecast next year's likely
equipment needs. She had already prepared a rough
list, but only last week the service engineer had con-
demned the two oldest shortwave diathermy machines.
She added their replacements to the list, while guessing
what the answer would be. 'If you're managing without
them at present, do you really need them at all, Miss
Fraser-Firth?'

In vain to point out that sufficient equipment and
staff meant quicker cures and sometimes saved in-
patient treatment. That was something the uninitiated
simply couldn't grasp. 'If I had my way I'd sack
everybody across the road——' Marnie glared at the
admin block '—and give back the power to the folk
with the responsibility. I wonder how the Government
would like to go to sea in a force-ten gale with a clerk
in charge of the ship?'

Doggedly she continued her list, making reasoned
arguments in favour of each item, while fairly certain
she was wasting her time. The allocation would be
about a quarter what was needed. The money for the
new admin block had got to come from somewhere!

By eleven Marnie had done her best and popped her
morning's labours into an envelope to be dropped off
in Admin on her way to the ward.

It was a relief to get down to some real work for a
change, and she spent a rewarding hour or more with
her ward patients before the lunches were brought in.
Then she and Sonia returned to Physio. 'I'll just fetch

my lunch,' said Sonia, but Belle said better not, as
Marnie had a visitor.

'Rather an important one,' she added.

Surely not the general manager, come to buy my
silence? thought Marnie. The idea had great possi-
bilities, but it was James she found lounging in her best
chair with the coffee made and enough food for an
army spread out on her desk. 'You're the last person I
expected to see,' she faltered, flushing to the roots of
her golden curls as last night's humiliating memories
came flooding back.

'Why?' he asked simply, getting up to pour out.

'Well—I mean to say. . .' she stumbled feebly.

'You think a written apology would have been
better.'

Marnie gasped with surprise. 'What do you have to
apologise for? I was the one who got drunk and talked
all manner of rubbish.'

'Not at all. I found your chatter rather endearing. As
for the rest, I was the one who kept refilling your glass.
Incidentally, you're wonderfully dignified when you're
fu',' he added. 'Did you know?'

'I am?' Marnie realised it would be easier to gaze in
wonder at him if she was sitting down. 'Well, I wasn't
too fu' to know I talked an awful lot of rot which I—I
hope you'll overlook—or better still, forget, and. . .'

'*In vino veritas*,' said James, sitting down again and
leaning forward, elbows on knees. 'As I recall, you
confessed to nothing worse than not sleeping around. I
don't see anything very dreadful in that—rather the
contrary. It shows common sense and good taste.'

'It does?'

'You don't agree?' he queried.

'I'm—just so amazed to hear you saying that.' James
winced. 'I mean, it's not that I'm suggesting. . . Just

that—you have such a kind way of summarising my drunken ramblings.'

'But then, as I keep pointing out, I am——'

'Kind. Yes, I know. And it's true,' Marnie agreed.

'Have a sandwich,' said James, proffering the box, 'and then tell me when we're going out again.'

'You'd really—risk it?'

'Never leave a job half done,' said James. 'I'm on call tonight——'

'And I've got a meeting.'

'So how about tomorrow?'

'You mustn't neglect real life in order to help me,' said Marnie firmly. 'I'm sure there must be other things you'd rather be doing.'

James stared at her through narrowed eyes for several seconds, as though trying to gauge what lay behind her resistance. In the end he said, 'I'll strike a bargain with you. If I get a better offer, then I'll stand you up. Otherwise, I'm told the new play at the King's is a laugh a minute.'

'But will anybody from the hospital be there?' asked Marnie, still wrestling with her decision to put a stop to this.

'I think I like you better when you're drunk,' said James. 'You certainly ask fewer questions. Now drink your coffee—it's getting cold.'

Today James was able to finish his lunch in peace before being called away to advise the registrar about treatment for a small boy who had fallen off the back of a lorry. 'Good grief, that's a new line in stolen goods!' said Marnie, when he told her why he was wanted.

They shared a smile at that; a second or so of warmth. Then James said gently, 'I have to go, Marnie. See you later, huh?'

'Of course. And thanks for lunch,' she called after him from the doorway as Belle came bustling up. She was carrying a pile of patients' records for sorting, and after looking at Marnie's littered desk she asked, 'So where shall I put these.'

Marnie scooped up the remains of lunch. 'Here, please, Belle. And as for all this——'

'Give it to me,' Belle instructed. 'I'll ask the nearest ward to keep it in their fridge overnight. Himself'll be back tomorrow, no doubt.'

'As to that——' began Marnie.

'I know it's none of my business,' said Belle, 'but I do hope all this is leading somewhere useful—like up the aisle. I like James Dalgleish, and it's my belief he's not half as bad as his unsuccessful female pursuers would have folk believe. So there!' And, having delivered herself of that weighty bit of opinion, Belle marched out and shut the door. She opened it again almost at once to tell Marnie she'd just seen Mr Montgomery coming in.

'Thanks, Belle,' Marnie returned absently. She'd been busy composing a not unpleasing mental picture of James at the altar, resplendent in Highland dress, and herself a vision in white, floating blissfully towards him on her father's arm. Are you out of your mind? she was asking herself next minute. No more than a fortnight ago you couldn't stand the sight of him. And this is all a game, remember. Real life is Dominic— and coping with people like Mr Montgomery.

Angus Montgomery had been treated by practically every physio on the staff before finding his way on to Marnie's list. Each time he made some progress, but never quite recovered. He was, she suspected, a professional patient who enjoyed his visits to hospital.

'So how's the back today, then, Mr Montgomery?' she enquired brightly.

'So-so, m'lass. Yesterday I was thinkin' we were almost there, then this morning I could hardly get out ma bed.'

He said more or less the same thing every time he came. 'You'll be pleased to know your check X-ray is normal, anyway,' Marnie told him.

'Ah, but bones is only the half of it. My trouble's mostly muscular, and muscles dinnae show up, right? I think I'm needin' some massage.'

'Here's something we haven't tried yet,' urged Marnie, uncovering the new machine on loan to them for assessment. 'Duntrune City's physio swears by it.' Mr Montgomery was a dedicated football fan.

'But mine's no' an injury, hen,' he returned firmly. He was nearly as good at having the last word as James Dalgleish.

On the ward that afternoon, Mrs Kerr was ready and eager. She'd just had a letter from her daughter in Canada, inviting her over for a holiday, all expenses paid. 'And I'll never get up the jumbo steps if my knee's not bending more than this, will I, dear? So I thought I'd just do a bit on my own till you came. Did I do right?'

'Wonderful, Mrs Kerr. Just what the doctor ordered,' smiled Marnie.

'He ordered elbow crutches and all, but I'm not wanting them.'

'They'd be much more convenient than a Zimmer— especially on a plane, Mrs Kerr.'

'D'you know, you've got a point there,' agreed the patient. 'Will we give it a whirl when we've done the exercises?'

'Splendid idea!' exclaimed Marnie, wondering if

there was any chance that Mr Montgomery had a daughter living halfway up the Matterhorn who would like him to visit.

Sonia was depressed. Basher wasn't walking any better, and James had noted more adverse signs in both legs on the ward-round that morning. 'He lives on the fourteenth floor of that tower block on the Eastside estate, where all the vandalism is, Marnie. How will he manage? He'll go mad, cooped up all day.'

'Now's the time to get the medical social worker on to the possibility of re-housing,' suggested Marnie. 'I'll give her a ring if you like. And then I could do some patients for you later—I've got almost half an hour to spare this afternoon.'

Sonia said it would be wonderful if Marnie could take the male knees, now that Sister had put them in the little ward where they'd be spotted if they tried to sneak off to the loo without their crutches. 'They're quite a decent lot. I don't think they'll tease you too much,' she added.

'Not to worry, Sonia, my back's broad.' Which was just what James had said when offering to act as fall guy when the face-saving campaign was wound up. I think about him far too much, Marnie realised. It's not sensible. In fact, it's asking for trouble. I've got to stop it.

Easier said than done. The knee patients might be quite a decent lot, but they weren't behind with the innuendoes, and it took all Marnie's histrionic powers to put on a pretence of innocence.

Then at the meeting after work, to which a small group of physios from all over Duntrune had come to plan next winter's lecture programme, Emily Craig suggested asking Mr Dalgleish to bring them up to date on all the latest techniques in orthopaedic surgery.

'He's very good, of course, but by no means the most senior orthopod in the city,' Marnie pointed out in her capacity as branch secretary.

'No, but he is the most charismatic,' put in the superintendent from the City Hospital. 'What's the betting we'd get a full turn-out to listen to him?'

Enthusiastic murmurs rippled all round the table. 'You *are* lucky, Marnie,' whispered the girl sitting next to her. 'And I don't mean because you're working in the same hospital.' She didn't work in a hospital at all, but in a school for physically handicapped children. The grapevine was even more widely spread than Marnie had realised.

The meeting broke up at half-past seven. Marnie disliked these after-work meetings that left one with half the evening to kill. Dominic was helping his boss to wine and dine some Japanese business men tonight, and as it was now raining heavily for the first time in weeks she couldn't even go for a walk. I'll go home, have supper and then work on my article for the *Journal* she decided.

But later, having got out her typewriter, Marnie found she couldn't settle. Her mind was playing tricks again. She made a coffee and had another go. 'The Changing Face of Physiotherapy', she typed. No, make it 'Physiotherapy—2000'. . .

She was gazing into space, feeling James caressing her bare back as he had last Saturday night in this very room. She found herself aching for him to repeat it, while scolding herself for such folly at the same time. Why could she not feel like that when Dominic touched her? All at once, Marnie was desperately afraid. 'I'd like to kill that man who left his van in front of my car!' she breathed. 'If he hadn't, none of this would have happened and I'd still be my normal, contented, unemotional self.'

When the doorbell rang, she found her bag and stuffed a pound into the charity envelope she'd found lying on the mat when she came in. When the bell rang a second time, she muttered, 'All right, all right, you'll get your money!' Then she opened the door and held out the envelope.

It was James standing there. He took the envelope and put it in the recess where the milkman left the milk. 'She's still working her way round the ground floor,' he said easily. 'Are you intending to keep me here all night? Sorry, perhaps I should qualify that. . .'

'Oh, come in,' said Marnie, standing aside, her thoughts and senses in chaos at his unexpected appearance. Fate really wasn't playing fair. Or could this be the opportunity she needed to break loose?

'Do you not want to know how I got in?' wondered James, coming in and shutting the door behind him.

'Andrew, I suppose.'

'Wrong, though that would have been useful. Actually, I met the envelope collector at the front door, and she recognised me from way back, when I treated her daughter for adolescent scoliosis. So she vouched for me when a dear little soul on the ground floor let us in. Who would that be, Marnie? She's obviously retaining fluid—her ankles were very swollen and she was breathless. She ought to see her doctor.'

'That'll be Mrs Swann. I'll make a point of calling on her and finding out the state of play.'

'Good girl!' He treated her to a thorough appraisal. 'You look absolutely wonderful in that loose thing.' 'That loose thing' was a multi-patterned kaftan she often wore at home. 'Full of Eastern promise,' he added softly.

Marnie thrilled to that before gathering her dignity and determination. 'I thought you were supposed to be on call tonight, James.'

'There's no supposition about it—I am. But as things have been very quiet so far, I gave your number to the junior reg in case of trouble and hied myself round here—where else? Anyway, you're that bit nearer to the dear old place than I am.' He frowned. 'Are you going to let me into your living-room, or have you got that Dominic character in there?'

'Dominic's dining with some Japanese clients tonight,' Marnie threw over her shoulder as she led the way. 'And I'm actually very glad you came round, because I want to talk to you. Very seriously.'

'I don't like the sound of that,' said James. 'Perhaps I ought to have a drink first.'

Marnie was already at the drinks table. 'Whisky?' she offered. 'I've got a twelve-year-old Islay malt here.'

'I'll look forward to that some night when I'm off duty. Tonic, please, with just a smidgen of gin to flavour. And I mean that. There's nothing more terrifying to a nervous patient than a surgeon smelling of booze.'

Marnie mixed herself a similar innocuous drink so as to have something to do while she decided what to say.

'To us,' said James, clinking glasses before she could stop him.

'That is what I want to talk about,' said Marnie, very firm, very determined.

'Oh, yes.' His grin had faded at her tone, leaving his face serious and wary. 'Go on,' he invited quietly when she didn't say anything more.

'When we started this—this charade,' she said hesitantly, 'you said a week or a fortnight should do it.'

'I remember.'

'But we seem to have got such tremendous coverage—even outside the Royal—so I think we could stop now.'

'You do?' For somebody usually so articulate, James was being no help at all.

'Yes, I do.' She paused, running a not too steady forefinger round and round the rim of her glass. 'You also said we could make it look as though I was the one to walk away. . .' Her voice petered out. James was frowning and looking anything but co-operative. 'You promised!' she said sharply.

He put down his glance and moved nearer. 'Have you really hated every moment we've spent together so much?' he asked quietly.

Whatever sort of reaction she'd expected, it wasn't that. 'Hated? No, of course not! But that's not the point.'

'So what is the point, then?'

The point was that Marnie was terrified of falling in love with him, with all the heartbreak and ridicule that would bring. 'We ought never to have started this in the first place,' she insisted. 'It was a crazy idea.'

'Thank you,' said James impassively.

'Well, it was,' she insisted. 'All we had to do was to ignore the rumour and let it die a natural death, not——'

'You've changed your tune since Saturday! You were scared silly for your image then.'

'I wasn't thinking straight then. Now I am. And I'm saying we should call a halt before any more damage is done.'

'Damage?' James considered that for a weighty minute. 'If this is a damage-limitation exercise, then this is about the worst possible time to stop it. Worse than if we'd never begun.'

'I don't see that,' insisted Marnie.

'Then let me spell it out for you. The idea was to show we had an ongoing relationship, right? Thus dispelling the idea of a one-night stand. Is calling a halt after a few days of high-profile dating going to do that? I think it would only increase speculation. The best thing to do is to carry on with the remedy until folk lose interest—as they will, when the next sensation comes along.'

'But what about—real life?' she asked.

His lip curled derisively. 'If by that you mean your yuppy boyfriend, then I'm bound to say that "real" is not an adjective I would apply to that relationship.'

'It may not be exactly—earth-moving, but it fills a— a gap. Still, I'll not argue the point.' Marnie didn't remember just how much she'd revealed last night. 'What about your own life?'

'If at this moment I were seriously involved with somebody, I'd hardly be in a position to have started this, would I? Do you suppose any woman would put up with it?'

'Certainly not—if she knew.'

'And as nobody sneezes at one end of Duntrune without repercussions at the other, I rest my case,' said James. 'Of course, if you're quite determined not to go out with me again, then there's not much I can do about it. I shall wonder why, though—when you've already admitted to enjoying it so far.'

Marnie didn't remember actually doing that, but it was difficult to think clearly when he was standing over her like this; so near and so compelling. *He's getting to me again,* she realised anxiously. *Somebody ring him up—please!*

Nobody did. 'There's a lot in what you say,' she had to admit. 'So I'll think about it.'

'Very sensible. And while you're thinking, do you mind if I put your telly on? I've not heard the news all day.' James didn't wait for agreement, but switched on and settled himself at ease in the corner of the sofa, long legs outstretched.

Marnie, who had foolishly expected him to leave, wasn't sure what to do next. 'Should I make coffee?' she wondered aloud.

James heard that. 'Lovely idea, sweetie—as long as it's not too much trouble.'

'Sit here,' he said, patting the sofa when Marnie came back. 'You'll not be able to see over there.'

Marnie very nearly said she didn't particularly want to, until she realised that the Health Service Minister was explaining the latest thinking on reorganisation, with illustrations.

Drinking coffee and listening to James's lucid and balanced views on the issue soon drifted gradually into relaxed conversation about all manner of things. James was deliberately low-profile now, encouraging her to talk and making her laugh. Just as he had the night before, except that Marnie was sober tonight.

All the time, the space between them had been getting smaller. Now the room was lit only by a soft orange glow diffusing upwards from the street lamps, and James's right arm was draped along the sofa back, almost brushing Marnie's shoulders.

'I think——' she began, just as he turned her gently towards him and kissed her just as gently.

A lovely warm glow pervaded her. She could no more have pulled away from him than taken wing. She could have stayed like that for ever, with thought and anxiety quite suspended.

The phone hadn't rung when she wanted it to, but it did now, and James released her with a groan. 'Perhaps it's only for me,' Marnie said hopefully, going to answer it. James went too. 'No, I'm afraid it's for you, James. A man has fallen off a ship on to the quay.'

He took the phone with a sigh of frustration, but his expression grew keen as he listened. 'All right—I'll be there in fifteen minutes,' he said crisply.

He replaced the phone and took Marnie in his arms again. 'I have to go,' he murmured against her hair.

'I know,' she whispered, unsure whether to be glad or sorry about this reprieve.

'But there's to be no more backsliding,' he insisted. 'Tomorrow we'll be picking up where we're leaving off tonight.' When she would have spoken, he stopped her mouth with a kiss. 'Till tomorrow, then—say it!'

'Till tomorrow,' she repeated, mesmerised.

CHAPTER EIGHT

MARNIE was crooning to herself in the shower, a little smile on her face. She smiled rather a lot these days, as Belle had remarked only yesterday with a satisfied little smile of her own.

Last night had been wonderful. James had taken her to the Riverside again; the first time there since their first date. 'After all, it is a sort of anniversary,' he'd said whimsically.

'Of what?' Marnie had asked, laughing.

'The laying of the first smokescreen.' They were keeping up that story. 'Exactly twenty-five days ago today.'

'What kind of an anniversary is that?' she had laughed in reply.

'Every day is an anniversary to me, sweetheart,' James had answered with that special look which always made her feel she was giving at the knees.

After dinner, they'd come back here and danced smoochily on her little terrace, pressed together, her head on his shoulder and his hands inside her blouse. Soon—very soon— it wouldn't stop there, and Marnie looked forward with a longing that was tinged with just a little bit of doubt. James was terrific; kind, thoughtful, amusing and very, very exciting, but she still hadn't the least idea how he really felt about her. He called her every endearment under the sun—except his love. Was he keeping that for the ultimate surrender—or was it simply that true love was not on the agenda?

Oh, to hell with it! she thought. Live for the day,

Marnie, be happy while you can and let the future bring what it will, she decided, as she stepped out of the shower and reached for a towel. Quite a change of heart for a girl who had lived for twenty-eight years considering the consequences of every move she made.

When the phone went, she felt sure it must be James. 'Well, hello, there,' she purred into it.

'Is that you, Marnie?' Sonia asked doubtfully in return.

Swiftly Marnie pulled herself together. 'You're not coming in today,' she assumed in her normal voice.

'Yes, I am,' said Sonia, 'but it'll be a big help if you can pick me up. My car died on me on the way home last night. I had to call the garage and they say the damn thing'll not be ready until tomorrow.'

'Of course I'll collect you—in about twenty minutes,' Marnie calculated. It would mean missing breakfast, but what did that matter when she was putting on pounds from all the lovely dinners James was giving her?

James. He was on call tonight, so they were eating at his place. He was, she had discovered, a wizard in the kitchen—just as he was everywhere else. What a good thing that Dominic was on that business trip to Paris this week. So far, she'd managed to keep him from suspecting, but it was getting more difficult as James stepped up what he persisted in calling the campaign.

Sonia was on the pavement in front of her trim semi, so as not to keep Marnie waiting. 'I do appreciate this,' she said as they drove off.

'You'd do the same for me,' returned Marnie confidently. 'Anyway, it's in my best interests to get my staff to work on time.'

'So where was it last night?' asked Sonia.

'The Riverside at Invertrune. You take a great interest in my social life, Sonia Graham.'

'I expect that's because I'm supposed to be your best friend.' A fractional pause. 'Marnie——'

Marnie anticipated the rest. 'You think I'm playing with fire, don't you? I know I am. But I'm not getting burned yet.'

'That's not what I was going to say. Did you know that James is supposed to have somebody else, somewhere? A long-term thing, I'm told; a sort of mutually convenient arrangement for two busy doctors. . .' Sonia, stopped, unhappy with the way she was sounding this warning.

'James has already told me there isn't anybody.' He'd implied in Duntrune, though, and here was Sonia saying 'somewhere'. . . 'Anyway, I can look after myself,' boasted Marnie, like countless others of her sex before her. Firmly she changed the subject. 'How's that nice husband of yours—and my wee godson, Fraser?'

'Wondering when you're coming for Sunday lunch again. How about this coming weekend?'

Marnie shook her head. 'Sorry, love. I'd really have liked that, but I have to fetch Dad from the airport.'

'So soon? Is it really six weeks since he went away?'

'Six weeks to the day, come Sunday,' confirmed Marnie. 'I wonder what today has in store for us?' she wondered as they turned in at the hospital gates.

Sonia had been silenced for now, but the little note of discord she'd sounded had not. Marnie went very thoughtfully about her work that morning. There was a lot to do—planning the next unit switch-round for the junior staff, drafting a convincingly worded request for funds to send physios on post graduate courses, giving a class of new student nurses their first insight into the workings of a physiotherapy department—and all interspersed with her own patients. Marnie had expanded her list when Lynne Selkirk returned to work and she was no longer needed to help out on the wards.

Now that he monopolised most of her evenings, James came less often for lunch, and Marnie was just settling down to a final polishing of that important request for funds when there was a knock on the door.

When she called out, 'Come in,' it was Fiona who entered.

'Why, hello,' said Marnie, sure that she knew what the girl wanted. 'I'd like you to spend your short time remaining on the medical unit, Fiona. As you know, the Western General gets lots of chest cases, so Michael will make sure you get a good variety.'

'Yes, about the Western,' said Fiona. 'I'm not sure I really want to go there now.'

Marnie swallowed a gasp of surprise. 'That's a pity— I'm not sure the transfer can be stopped at this late stage.'

Fiona shrugged. 'All right—I s'pose I'll have to go, then. Only I really do like it here. I'm a nuisance,' she concluded.

Marnie didn't see how she could deny that. 'I'll ask Personnel how far they've got with the paperwork,' she promised. 'May I ask you why you've changed your mind?'

'Now that I'm back with Joe, things look very different.' I'll bet they do, thought Marnie, who hadn't heard that snippet of news. 'It was really stupid of me to get so worked up about that crush I had on James Dalgleish. Apart from anything else, he's much too old for me.' Fiona was looking quite embarrassed. 'And he didn't really lead me on as much as I made out,' she confessed in a rush.

Marnie wasn't to be drawn into discussing James. 'I'm very glad to hear that you're back on an even keel, Fiona, but things are out of my hands now. I'll do what I can to keep you here, but I can't promise anything.' She picked up her pen to show that the interview was over.

'I know you will, Marnie. You always do your best for us.'

What a change since we last talked, thought Marnie, wondering why Fiona was still standing there, looking slightly uncomfortable and fiddling with the stethoscope in her pocket.

'I've simply got to tell you something,' Fiona blurted out at last. 'You'll probably be mad, but I've got to. It's for your own good.'

Not another one who thinks she knows what's best for me! 'All right, so what do you want to tell me, then?' asked Marnie.

'It's about James's doctor friend in Glasgow. She's a paediatrician, and it's been going on for years and years. He told me all about her as one way of trying to prise me loose. He said they had this thing going and might even get married some day—before they got too old and lonely. Oh, Marnie, I had to tell you, because I'll bet he hasn't! And it's only right you should know what you're up against. I talked it over with some of the girls——' Oh, God! '—and they agreed I ought to. We're all very fond of you, you know, and we'd hate to see you get hurt.'

Marnie stopped doodling on the memo pad and looked at Fiona with all the serenity she could conjure up. 'I do know about her, as it happens—and also exactly what I'm doing.' She allowed herself a little smile. 'This is in confidence, mind, but I'm sure you'll agree that it's high time that the gentleman in question was taught a little lesson.'

Fiona's eyes grew rounder still. 'Gosh, Marnie, I never thought of that. How clever! I can't wait to see his face when he finds out!'

'In confidence, mind,' Marnie repeated, aghast at the way she'd let her tongue run away with her. She'd had no idea she would say that.

'Cross my heart,' responded Fiona, dashing off, big with news.

As soon as the door closed behind her, Marnie stopped pretending. She slumped in her chair and tried to come to terms with that second bombshell. She didn't doubt the truth of it for a moment. Back with her boyfriend and once more her former happy, carefree self, why should Fiona make up such a story? Besides, it tied in perfectly with Sonia's warning that very morning. Sonia might have gleaned her information from staff-room whispers, but it was more likely she'd heard it up on Ortho, where they probably knew where James used to sneak off to on his weekends off, before he started this idiotic campaign.

When James had told her he wasn't deeply involved with anyone, he had implied in Duntrune, and she had been satisfied. She'd never dreamed he had a compliant lover tucked away at a convenient distance, leaving him free to pursue other females on his home ground. Trust him to have everything worked out so neatly; it was part of his all-round efficiency.

And now she had to find the strength and conviction to end this farce once and for all. Today. Tonight. But first there was the afternoon to get through.

'Yon fancy box o' tricks is making us worse, hen,' claimed Mr Montgomery. 'It's spread to ma hands now, and ma feet's gone all numb. And my glasses is needin' changin'. I reckon I should be gettin' massage.'

Marnie struggled to connect all that up scientifically, and gave up. Massage was the one thing she hadn't tried, because she didn't see how it could help. But since his condition defied diagnosis, why be logical about treatment? 'Strip to your underpants and lie face downwards on the couch, then, Mr Montgomery,' she instructed. 'I'll be back in a second.'

Mrs McAndrew was back for a second course of treatment, unable to grasp that being pain-free didn't mean you could go straight back to all the bad old ways that had crippled you in the first place. Or maybe it was her husband who didn't understand. There were so many ways in which a man could hurt a woman. Rab McAndrew and James Dalgleish between them were making Dominic seem like a prince. Marnie insisted to herself that she was really looking forward to their reunion when Dominic got back from Paris.

At least Mr Scott was a success story. Only four treatments, and already his back was better than it had been for years. *And* he'd had two courses of treatment from an osteopath before trying the NHS as a last resort. 'May I have a signed statement of competence, then, please, Mr Scott?' Marnie asked brightly. Never let your private troubles impinge on your professional life.

'My dear Miss Fraser-Firth, I'm ready to write to every newspaper in the land, but will this do to be going on with?' He produced champagne and Belgian chocolates from his real leather briefcase. Gordon Scott owned Scotia Electronics and was widely believed to be a millionaire. He was also just on the wrong side of fifty, but still quite dishy. 'I'd rather ask you out to dinner, but I suppose that must wait until I'm no longer your patient,' he purred.

'Oh, absolutely,' returned Marnie, dimpling suitably. She knew for a fact that he was married, but, as the invitation would probably never materialise and she would contrive to be busy if it did, she could afford to be pleasant now. 'Can you manage the same time tomorrow?' she was asking when somebody hit the panic button in the gym. ''Scuse me!' she rapped out, pushing past him out of the cubicle and racing down the corridor.

A man lay on his back in the middle of the floor, with two scared-looking young juniors struggling to loosen his collar. All the other patients had paused, awestruck, in their exercises—a still life, action suspended.

Dreading what she would find, Marnie dropped to her knees beside the motionless figure. 'Jane, buzz the arrest team! Betty, the airway for mouth-to-mouth!' she ordered, raising the patient's legs in the air for a second or two, to get the blood flowing back to the heart, before striking him a smart blow in the middle of the chest. Then she began cardiac massage, alternating with Betty's artificial respiration.

It seemed hours instead of minutes—it always did— before the resuscitation team arrived hotfoot to take over.

'Get all the other patients over to the antenatal room,' Marnie whispered to Betty.

'But most of 'em are men,' returned Betty, trembling with shock.

Marnie laid a calming hand on her shoulder. 'Let's just get them all out, shall we? And back to work as soon as possible. This way, please, everyone,' she said coolly.

'But there's no equipment in that room.'

'Then take what you can carry or push in a wheel-chair. Improvise. We're in the way here now, Betty.'

By the time the alternative scenario had been set up, Marnie had two more of her own patients waiting for treatment. And now the crisis was past and the collapsed patient was being wheeled out on a trolley. His face was uncovered. 'Thank God!' she breathed.

'Aye, ye did a good job there, miss,' said one of the porters who was wheeling him.

'All in the day's work,' returned Marnie. 'Right, Mr Paterson, so how are you today?'

'All the better for seeing you, Miss Firth.'

So things were back to normal—on the work front, at least. But things were far from normal in her private life, and Marnie was dreading the evening.

Marnie took longer than usual getting ready that night; partly because she wanted to look her best, but more because she needed time to decide how best to play out the final scene. Somehow, she must get James to tell her about his Glasgow girlfriend. But how? I'll just have to keep my wits about me and watch out for the least chance, she decided unhappily. But I've got to find out. And then with a little spurt of relief she told herself that perhaps it was all over between them. Perhaps he had been telling her the whole truth when he said there was nobody. Perhaps it had been finished before he took up with her.

But Marnie was no fool, and she had to admit that wasn't likely. It would be just too tidy and convenient altogether. And most of the time life was neither the one nor the other.

All this fretting and thinking had taken time, and Marnie was later than she'd said she'd be getting to

James's neat little mews house, tucked away in a row behind the great Victorian mansions which fronted the river. Once, they had been the homes of the ship-owners and merchants who had made Duntrune the city it was. Now, most of them had been turned into offices.

She parked on the cobbles in front of James's kitchen window, and he had the door open before she could ring. 'Darling, what kept you? I was getting really worried.' He had a saucepan in one hand, but he pulled her towards him with the other and kissed her warmly, a kiss she instinctively returned and promptly regretted.

'Oh, this and that,' she returned vaguely. 'You know how it is.' She had bought a jar of his favourite pâté before today's unwelcome developments, and she put it on the hall table. 'Just something for the store cupboard,' she said dismissively.

He picked it up, obviously pleased by the gift. 'This is very sweet of you, but you shouldn't have.' He leaned down to kiss her again, but, with both hands full now, he couldn't capture her when she moved into the kitchen, asking, 'Is there anything I can do to help?'

'Not now, sweetie, it's all done. Or will be when I've poured this sauce over the fish.'

'Fish?' she queried.

'I got some turbot.'

'James, how wildly extravagant!'

'Nothing is too good for you, my angel.' Except, perhaps, his undivided affection! Marnie was glad she'd thought of that. It helped her to ask lightly, 'So when were the TV cameras installed, then?'

James finished coating the fish and returned it to the

oven to keep warm before turning to her with a frown. 'What have cameras got to do with anything?' he asked.

'All this——' Marnie waved a hand over the table set with flowers and candles '—and nobody to see and report—unless we're under surveillance.

'Ah!' said James, with emphasis. 'I want to talk to you about that.' His voice softened, taking on a caressing note. 'Is it not about time we abandoned all this pretence?'

As recently as this morning, Marnie would have seen that as the sign she'd been waiting for. In the light of the day's revelations, she wasn't so sure. 'If you say so—after all, you were the one who insisted on keeping it going.'

Now it was his turn to be puzzled. 'What exactly did you think I meant?' he asked.

'That this farce has gone on long enough.'

'I didn't say farce, Marnie, I said pretence.'

They seemed to be going round in circles. 'Farce, pretence—what's the difference?'

'That depends,' he said. He was looking at her anxiously now. It was the first time Marnie had ever seen him less than confident. Could he possibly be feeling guilty? How she wished she had the courage to probe!

'Do you realise you haven't offered me a drink yet?' she asked with a nervous little laugh.

James's frown lessened and the tension that had been building between them slackened a bit. 'What a rotten host I am!' he exclaimed. 'Letting myself get bogged down in semantics like that. What'll it be, then, darling? Gin and tonic? That always seems to suit you.'

That's right, she thought. Get me sozzled and blunt my reasoning powers! 'Let me mix the drinks,' she said quickly. 'I've done nothing yet to earn my dinner.' She went straight into the living-room and over to the drinks cupboard before he could say no. James followed, bringing lemon and ice.

'You're being very mean with the gin,' he said, taking the bottle out of her hand and pouring more.

'James! You're on call,' she warned.

'No, I'm not. Andrew wanted to swap because he's got something on tomorrow night. And it doesn't make much difference to us. Incidentally, I think I told you I have to go to Glasgow on Saturday, but I should be back by teatime.'

She'd never get a better chance than this. 'I didn't know you were going to Glasgow,' she pounced.

'Surely I told you I had a meeting?'

'I remember that, but I don't recall hearing it was in Glasgow.' She took a big breath. 'The shops there are so much better than ours, so why don't I come with you and spend a lot of money while you're in your meeting?'

James was looking ill at ease for the second time that evening. 'I'm—not sure that's a very good idea, darling. It could take ages, or it might not. So——'

'It sounds a very odd sort of meeting to me,' she said.

He took refuge in bluster, asking angrily, 'What's that supposed to mean?'

'Only that one usually has some idea how long meetings are likely to last.'

'But in this case, I have not.'

Marnie took a long swig at her drink before going for the big one. 'I don't believe you've got a meeting at all,' she challenged. 'I think you're going to see another woman.' Thank heaven that had come out just right; sort of jokey.

James hesitated. He hesitated just too long before

claiming, 'You're the only woman in my life now, Marnie.'

She could no longer doubt what she'd been told that morning, but he mustn't guess how desolate, how hurt she was. 'Wonderful!' she said satirically. 'But for how long, I wonder?'

'That depends entirely on you,' he said quietly.

Yesterday she'd probably have thrown her arms round him for that. Now she contrived a brittle little laugh. 'Oh, James, what a decision! I shall have to give the matter a great deal of thought.'

He was obviously unhappy at her manner, but he chose to answer her words. 'Do that, Marnie—but please don't take too long about it. The suspense is—not easy to bear.'

'Twenty-four hours should do it,' she pretended.

'Then you'll tell me over dinner tomorrow night?'

'But you'll be on call then—and so shall I,' she invented. 'I haven't taken a turn for ages.' Not since the night that ruddy van parked in front of my car and turned my life upside down. Oh, God! How much longer can I keep this up? Why did I come here at all, after——?

'What rotten planning, when you knew I was off this coming weekend,' said James. 'Still, it's turned out all right. We'll have an early supper together at the Waterman in the midst of our labours. And talking of supper, tonight's will be ruined if we don't have it soon.'

Somehow Marnie got through the meal, though she refused to drink much wine. She needed a clear head to cope with James afterwards. There must be no getting carried away tonight. Not now she knew all about his long-time girlfriend, mistress, lover or whatever she called herself.

James had long since recovered from his earlier lapse of confidence, seeming almost to take it for granted that all was settled to everybody's satisfaction.

Oh, yes, very handy, thought Marnie, watching him grinding coffee beans. A tame comforter here in Duntrune to provide your basic needs in between visits to your busy love in Glasgow. I suppose it's her precious career that keeps her there. By thinking such thoughts, she was building up an armour of anger on which she was counting to see her through.

He'll be thinking he's made a good choice in me, she thought. Another dedicated career girl with no apparent wish for anything more than a part-time private life! For a moment, Marnie was tempted to tell him she'd done her thinking, the answer was yes—and when would he like to get married? It would almost be worth it to see his shock and horror. Except that her self-esteem depended on not letting him know she'd ever taken him seriously—even for a moment.

She could feel her face contorting with emotion. She got up abruptly from the table and hurried through to the living-room.

James came after her. 'You're very quiet, my sweet,' he said in a troubled voice.

'It's not that easy to compete with a coffee grinder,' she returned without turning round. 'James, I really mustn't be late tonight. I have to be up very early tomorrow.'

'Why?' he asked, as she should have foreseen he would.

'I'm—I'm expecting the plumber.' Fool! Why didn't you say you had to pick up Sonia? she asked herself.

'I'm not sure I like taking second place to the plumber,' he said whimsically.

'The two of you are not exactly in competition,' was

the best she could come up with, turning to face him, hoping she could bear that.

'Fulfilling as we do quite different needs in your life,' he suggested softly.

'I've certainly never been wined and dined by my plumber, nice as he is. He's a respectable married man.'

'Whereas I'm unmarried—and available,' said James, his eyes holding hers.

'Also "mad, bad and dangerous to know",' she threw out.

But she couldn't hope to fend him off with words much longer, and that last effort had been a serious miscalculation. James covered the distance between them in one bound, pulling her into his arms and forcing her close. 'What do I have to do to convince you you don't have to go on fighting me?' he asked against her hair. He put a hand under her chin and raised her face to his. 'Don't you know you're driving me nuts?' he said in a voice that shook. His kiss was eager, forcing her lips apart, while his hands explored her body.

Marnie moaned—not from pleasure, but from fear that she wouldn't hold out, but James was not to know that. His kisses grew more urgent. She could sense his arousal. There was to be no drawing back tonight.

With all her will-power she stamped hard on his foot, breaking free when he relaxed his hold in that moment of astonishment.

'You think you're irresistible!' she hissed. 'Well, you're not! I wouldn't go to bed with you if you were the last man on earth!' And with that, she ran outside to her car. She pulled at the door, wrenching and shaking, but it was locked and the keys were inside the house—in her bag, with her house keys. 'Damn, damn,

damn,' she whimpered as tears of anguish and mortification coursed down her cheeks.

Something landed with a thud on the roof of the car, making her jump. Her bag. She looked round and saw James standing in the doorway, his face dark. 'You only had to say no,' he gritted between lips that were stiff with anger.

'Oh—go to Glasgow!' she shouted, but by then he'd gone in and slammed the door.

Marnie opened her bag with trembling hands and found her car keys. She drove away, after crashing the gears and narrowly missing an old horse trough filled with flowers. She was numb with misery.

CHAPTER NINE

MARNIE had arranged to pick up Sonia again this morning, as Sonia's car wouldn't be ready until noon. 'I did it last night,' she said awkwardly as they drove away.

Sonia was thinking about her small son who was cutting a back tooth and would be giving his granny a bad time today. 'Did what, Marnie?' she asked abstractedly.

'Gave James his marching orders. It seemed best to do it before Dad came home and started asking awkward questions. He'd never have understood that crazy arrangement.'

'That's true. So how did he take it?'

'He was very angry,' said Marnie.

'I'll bet! This must be the first time that's ever happened to him.' Sonia cast a quick sidelong glance at her friend. 'And how do you feel, Marnie?'

'Me?' Marnie changed into a lower gear and turned left. 'Rather relieved, really. It was great fun while it lasted, but it had to end some time. It was getting in the way of real life. Oh, this traffic! If they don't build a ring-road soon. . .' She felt she'd handled that well. She'd planned to tell Sonia during this drive, partly because coping with the traffic could account for any awkwardness on her part, and also because she wouldn't have to look Sonia in the face—and vice versa. Sonia could be relied on to let the news filter out as appropriate, and spare her any awkward questions from her staff.

'Dominic comes back today, does he not?' asked Sonia. 'Are you sure he hasn't guessed?'

'Fairly sure. He's been so busy with this international deal.'

'So it's the mixture as before, then.'

'That's right. Did you see the way that red Ford cut in? Now if a woman had done that. . .'

By the time Marnie had shut herself in her office, she was trembling with the effort of trying to seem her normal, unruffled self. Thank heaven today was Friday. If she could just keep up the act today, then she'd have the weekend in which to recover. She peered at her reflection in the mirror over the washbasin. Yes, she'd made a pretty good job of disguising the dark circles under her eyes with make-up, but the eyes themselves looked awful after all the crying she'd done. Stop feeling sorry for yourself, you idiot, she scolded herself, or you'll start again, and Belle will be in with the post any minute.

Marnie had changed into uniform and was writing busily when Belle came. She braced herself to cope with her secretary's usual morning curiosity, but today Belle was too full of indignation about the state of the waiting-room floor. 'And the rest'll be just as bad, Marnie. If this place has so much as seen a mop these past three days, I'll—I'll. . .'

'I'll ring the domestic superintendent, Belle,' Marnie promised.

'And give it to her straight,' advised Belle, going out, still fuming.

Marnie intended to, just as soon as Mrs Wood was available, which wouldn't be yet. Go and see if Jock Kerr is in, then. He really should be taking things easily, with that back of his, but he was convinced that his firm would collapse without him, so Marnie treated him on his way to work each morning. 'How are things today?' she asked.

'Not too good, lass.'

'Then come and have some soothing electrical treatment before I manipulate you.' And while he was having that, she would see what was to be done with Mrs Bruce's funny shoulder.

Mrs Bruce was on her way home from her job as an office cleaner. 'I'm not over impressed with the state of this floor, Miss Firth,' she said, eyeing it scornfully.

'Me neither, Mrs Bruce, but not everybody has our standards, I'm sorry to say. Cubicle seven today, when you're ready. . .'

Marnie had just sent Mrs Bruce away feeling more comfortable and was thinking of tackling Jock Kerr's back when Belle came to tell her there was somebody from Admin on her office phone. Admin on the phone at this hour? Somebody was keen.

'Hi, Marnie,' said a breezy masculine voice that reminded her of a chat show host. 'We've not met, but I'm Don Revell, the new assistant chief personnel officer. Hi!'

You certainly are, thought Marnie grimly as she said, 'Good morning.'

'About that vacant post of yours, Marnie.'

'Actually, I have two vacancies on my staff, Mr Revell.'

'The thing is, we're interviewing the applicants today week at two. OK?'

'You may have difficulty getting hold of a consultant at that time,' warned Marnie. 'And may I remind you that he or she must be a mainstream physician or surgeon who uses physiotherapy a lot and knows what's needed in this hospital?' Last time, they'd tried to co-opt a part-time dermatologist for the panel.

'Is that a fact? No sweat, though. Everybody likes to knock off early on a Friday. OK?'

Ignoring what people said to you was certainly one way of coping. 'I've made a note of that, Mr Revell. Thanks for calling.'

'Great! Nice to get acquainted, Marnie.'

Where do they find them? she wondered as she rang off, to dial the domestic superintendent's number. Mrs Wood said grandly that she was reviewing the whole question of Marnie's floors, which left Marnie totally bewildered.

In and out of the office all morning, making phone calls and answering letters in between treatments. 'No wonder you're so slim, dear,' laughed the head porter, who had dropped in for a bit of advice because his feet were killing him. 'You're never still for a minute!'

The day limped by with neither sight nor sound of James—and no whisper of a rumour either. Marnie knew that, having made a point of going to the staff changing-room at the end of the day on the pretext of checking that the joiner had been to fix a faulty window latch. 'Have a good weekend, girls,' she wished them.

'You too, Marnie. And don't do anything we wouldn't,' called Jane, causing giggles all round.

'That gives me plenty of scope,' Marnie called back as expected. No, they definitely hadn't heard a whisper—yet.

She was on her way down the main corridor that led to the car park when she saw James coming out of Accident and Emergency surrounded by his junior doctors, who were listening respectfully to what he was saying. Almost as though he could feel her glance, James turned his head and saw Marnie. Then with a brief word to his team, he swung round on his heel and went back, leaving them to continue without him.

Marnie dashed into the hospital shop and bought a magazine she never read, rather than meet the doctors head-on. She hung on there, talking to the assistant until they'd passed. Thank heaven that had happened at the end of the day and not at the beginning. Oh, James, James, why could you not have felt for me what I feel for you? she thought sadly.

That evening, Marnie waited until nine before ringing Dominic. He would, by now, have had time to unpack and unwind with a shot of his favourite vodka and tonic. 'Dominic? Marnie here.'

'Why, hello, dear. How thoughtful of you to ring.'

'Not at all dear—I've missed you. How was Paris?'

'Very hot and smelly, but we clinched the deal.' Who but Dominic could so describe that lovely city—even in August?

'How trying for you—but I'm glad to hear about the deal.'

'Yes, this will look very good on my CV. Am I right in thinking there's a concert tomorrow night, dear?'

'Yes, you are, Dominic.'

'Good. Shall we meet at the usual time, then?'

'Lovely. Till tomorrow, then.'

'Till tomorrow. Goodnight, dear—so nice to hear your voice.' But not nice enough for him to chat on and on, making me laugh as—— Oh, stop it, you fool! That's your Saturday evening taken care of. Try to be grateful for that.

On Sunday, she'd be driving to Glasgow to meet her father home from his trip to the States. And James was going to Glasgow tomorrow, to visit his long-time lover. A fiery shaft of jealousy pierced Marnie when she thought of her. How she envied that unknown woman her possession of the only man she had ever wanted. Marnie strove not to picture them together, then in desperation she dialled Dominic's number again, ready to ask—no, beg him—to come round. But this time there was no reply.

So Marnie mooned about the flat, unable to settle to anything, until it got dark. Then she went to bed with a thriller. But it wasn't crime she dreamed of, but James at his most delightful and tender, and she woke next morning with a face that was wet with tears.

Saturday was awful; trying to keep busy with domestic chores and desperate all the time not to think of James with his lover. The evening was better, though, going to the concert with Dominic. During the interval, she kept glancing round, hoping to see somebody from the hospital who would relay the news that she was out with another man, but there was no one. And all she got was a reproof from Dominic for inattention. 'I'm telling you how I finally persuaded Heinrich Kleinson, dear, but if I'm boring you. . .'

'No, of course not, dear. It's fascinating.' She'd listened dutifully after that and all through supper at Gigli's as well. When the waiter brought the bill, Dominic took her money, so he'd not be groping her tonight. Marnie was glad. Now that she knew how it felt to warm to and want a man, she might very well have lost her temper.

Professor Fraser-Firth's plane was due in at eleven on Sunday morning, but was delayed for more than an hour by strong headwinds. In the instant before he saw her, Marnie thought he looked tired and sad, and she ached for him. Although he always insisted that he was quite content with his work, she knew he had never fully come to terms with her mother's death, three years before.

Later, over lunch at a small inn not far from the airport, Marnie put to him the idea that had been growing in her mind these past forty-eight hours.

'I re-stocked your fridge-freezer yesterday, Dad,' she began.

'That was thoughtful of you, darling.'

'Heavens, it was no trouble. Only I did some thinking while I was at it. That's a gey great house for you to rattle around in alone. . .'

He sighed. 'Yes, I know, but somehow I can't bring myself to leave it for something smaller. Your mother did so love that house. . .' He gestured helplessly.

'I know, Dad, and I wasn't suggesting that you should. What I'm trying to say is that it seems rather silly for me to keep my flat on when you've got so much room. So why do I not——'

'No, Marnie! We had all this out when she died. I will not allow you to give up your independence for me. You have your own life to lead.'

And a richt guid mess I'm making of it too! Marnie hesitated, wondering how to put her next point. 'I sometimes get lonely too,' she told him at last.

'You do?' Obviously that idea had never crossed his mind, but then why would it? It was a new one for Marnie herself. Her father's eyes brightened. 'You've broken with Dominic Keith,' he assumed.

'No, Dad. We're still the good friends we always were,' returned Marnie, disgesting the fact that her father didn't like Dominic. Never before, either by word or look, had he shown that.

'Forgive me, dear,' he said.

'It was the natural thing to think,' she excused him.

'So what is wrong, then?' he wondered. 'Have you got problems at work?'

Oh, my darling father, if you only knew! 'No more

than usual. You know how it is—never enough staff or equipment. . .'

'Don't we all? If it didn't mean our patients worrying themselves sick about the cost of being sick, I'd say there was something to be said for the American system. If you could only see those operating theatres, Marnie——' The professor stopped himself. 'But I was saving my experiences for later. Over supper at home, perhaps—as long as you haven't got something on.'

'On your first night home after so long? Not likely! I'm giving you roast beef and apple pie.' His favourite meal.

'You mustn't be too nice to me, or I might weaken and allow you back into the nest,' he said, smiling.

'That, my precious parent, was the general idea,' said his daughter as the waiter brought the bill.

Marnie stayed that night at her father's house, sleeping in her old room, which was full of memories of her secure and happy childhood. It was comforting, but not nearly comforting enough to ease her aching heart.

James was the first person she saw at the hospital next morning. He was talking on the front steps to Dr Robert Leith, senior physician and lifelong friend of her father's. Immediately she changed direction, but too late. She had already been spotted, and when Robert Leith called out to her she had to respond.

She said a nervous hello to James, who nodded gravely back as Rob asked. 'Did Fergus get home safely yesterday, Marnie?'

'Yes, thanks. And he really enjoyed the trip. Apparently the Americans were very kind about his lectures.'

Rob snorted. 'A man of his brilliance has no business to be so modest. Dora's phoning him later to fix dinner some time very soon.' He looked from Marnie to James and back, getting only an awkward silence in response. Wisely he let it drop, saying Sister Morrison would never forgive him if he was late for the ward-round. 'Yes, it's all go, is it not?' asked Marnie, beaming fatuously at her father's old friend, before dashing off herself. Heaven knows what he's thinking, she thought as she pelted down the corridor to Physio. Neither of us with a thing to say for ourselves. And there'd be other such awkward encounters, no doubt. She must try to be prepared next time.

Marnie wasn't though, because it came too soon. 'That was Outpatients on the line for you,' called Belle somewhere around the middle of the morning. 'You're wanted there now if not sooner, to see a new patient, but I told them you were in the middle of a manipulation and would come as soon as you'd finished.'

Marnie thanked Belle for her thoughtfulness.

'They fairly keep you busy, hen,' said the patient, intent on extending that unexpected rest with some conversation. 'And here was I thinking you were the high heid yin. In my line, it's all port and cigars and expensive lunches for the bosses.'

'I'm glad I'm not in your line, then,' said Marnie, forcing a smile. 'That doesn't sound like me at all. Now then, over on your front for the last manoeuvre.'

His treatment completed, Marnie did go to OP as requested.

'You'll find Mr Dalgleish in room four, Marnie,' said Sister.

'Um—thanks,' muttered Marnie, taken aback. It was customary for surgeon and therapist to see a patient together if there was any doubt about suitability for manipulation, but now that they had quarrelled Marnie would have expected James to get around that.

Reluctantly she tapped on the door, and quaked when he barked savagely.

'Come in!'

He looked formidable and completely out of reach, and Marnie's heart sank further. 'I—I'm sorry I couldn't come at once,' she said feebly, 'but I'm really terribly busy this morning.'

'Who isn't?' he asked curtly. 'But it's only the unit general manager you've kept waiting about in there.' A jerk of his curly dark head in the direction of the examination cubicle.

Mr Cooper, no less. No wonder James was giving him the full treatment! But was he remembering, as she was, the last time they'd seen him together, out at Lednoch House? If so, he gave no sign as he spelt out the details of the traffic accident in which Mr Cooper had hurt his back. 'Now he has limitation of movement and increasing pain with some radiation. He was thinking of going to an osteopath, but I told him to save his money. Now you'd better come and see what you make of him.' He led the way and then said, 'Miss Fraser-Firth wishes to apologise for keeping you waiting, George.'

'How kind,' said the UGM, still very much on his dignity, despite wearing nothing but the regulation tie-on cotton briefs.

'Mr Dalgleish has explained to me what happened, but I would just like to try one or two exploratory movements. . .' Marnie told him.

That done, she turned to James. 'May I see the films now, please?'

'Through here.' He waved her back into the consulting-room.

Marnie switched on the viewing screen and looked carefully. 'I can see a slight misalignment at D7/8 and

again at D11/12.' Her delicately arched brows drew
together. These double ones were always tricky. She
peered closer, and James handed her a magnifying
glass. Their hands touched in the change-over and he
pulled away as though he'd been stung.

Marnie re-mustered her concentration. 'Yes, as I
thought—the spinous process of the eleventh dorsal
vertebra looks to have an old malformation,' she said
unsteadily. 'Would that be congenital?'

'It would. Well, can you help him?'

'I think so. I'll certainly try.'

'I'd do better than that if you can,' he said. 'If you
cure him, you could probably screw those two extra
posts you're wanting out of him.'

Again she was reminded of that evening at Lednoch
House, and James's hilarious plans for blackmail. One
look at his gloomy expression told her that nothing was
further from his thoughts, now. 'I'd hate to think that
staffing my department depended solely on my curing
the general manager's back pain,' she said quietly.

'Have you any idea how sanctimonious that
sounded?' James asked coldly.

A bitter retort rose to her lips, but she controlled it.
'If it did, then I'm surprised. It certainly wasn't meant
to.' She allowed herself a stiff little smile. 'But if I am
successful, that's bound to improve his opinion of
physiotherapy.'

'Same sentiment, different wrapping,' reckoned
James.

That had been deliberate provocation. 'Fortunately,
I'm not particularly interested in your opinion of
me——' what a lie! '—and certainly not when I have
patients waiting. May I go and arrange Mr Cooper's
first appointment now, please?'

'Why not?' he asked savagely. 'That's why you're here!'

Not surprisingly, Marnie found it very difficult to concentrate after that. Clearly James was still smarting from her rejection of him, and that surprised her. Hadn't he had his usual supply of consolation over the weekend? But the patients were piling up, she found, when she got back to base. At this rate she'd be lucky to grab even half a sandwich before Mr Cooper came for his first treatment at one.

Marnie found treating George Cooper rather embarrassing. And he was obviously embarrassed too. We're both remembering that evening, she guessed. All the same, he was improving—or said he was. By Wednesday, and his third treatment, he claimed to be almost pain-free.

'I'm amazed,' she said frankly. 'I'd have expected it to take at least a week before you felt the benefit.'

'I'm entirely in your hands as regards the length of the course,' he insisted, 'but I am much better, and I'm very grateful. Especially when you're so busy. This place is like a Sunday market! Have I struck a bad week?'

Marnie seized her chance. 'No, this is par for the course. I did put in for two more posts last year to take account of increased workloads, but I was told that was out of the question, with the new offices to be staffed.' She gave him her most brilliant smile and watched him reel. 'So, somehow, we soldier on—and taking my paperwork home with me is often more entertaining than watching the box.' Not that she'd done much of either lately.

'I'd no idea things were quite so fraught at grass-roots level,' he said. 'If you could burn the midnight oil yet again and give me some facts and figures to back up your claim, I'll look into the matter.'

She'd done that, more than once, so Marnie decided not to believe Christmas had come early until she saw some results, but she told him she'd be very grateful for anything he could do to help.

Wednesday turned out to be a milestone in other ways too. Fiona arrived back from the wards just as George Cooper was leaving, and she hung about to say, 'Congratulations, Marnie. I knew you could do it!'

'Yes, he's a lot better, is he not?' asked Marnie watching the UGM striding briskly away.

Fiona then burst into giggles, told Marnie she was really, really cool and went skipping off towards the staff-room.

I'll never understand that girl, thought Marnie, going into her office, where Sonia was waiting.

'So I owe you a fiver,' said Sonia, 'but I hope you'll wait for it till payday. I've just had a thumping great garage bill for last week's breakdown.'

'I'll need to know what you're talking about before I agree,' said Marnie. 'I hope salmon and cucumber suits Your Majesty.' It was her turn to bring the sandwiches.

'I'd been hoping for caviare,' said Sonia drolly, 'but do you mean to say you really haven't heard? Ortho's fairly buzzing!'

Marnie was hit by a wave of utter despair. Had James decided to regularise his relationship with his Glasgow friend—or taken up with Helen Ballantyne again? She collapsed rather than sat down at her desk. 'I'm stuck in the department all day, so how would I get to hear anything?' she wailed, contriving to make it all look like an act.

'He's done it,' said Sonia. 'And I said he wouldn't, if

you remember. Of course, if you don't, then I'll hang on to my money.'

'Sonia, if you don't tell me whatever it is in plain English, I think I'll probably kill you!' warned Marnie, unable to stand the suspense a moment longer. 'Who's done what?'

'James has let it be known that you've dumped him—just as he promised you he would. And d'you know? I found myself feeling really sorry for him when I heard. It takes guts for a man to admit a thing like that.'

'Yes, indeed,' agreed Marnie, because she was so relieved that he wasn't getting married. 'Now let's hope for everybody's sake that the ruddy grapevine will soon find something else with which to—to choke itself.'

Now she also understood Fiona's cryptic remarks. Right now, she was probably regaling the girls with the story of how it was all a deliberate plan on Marnie's part to teach James a lesson. Please, dear God, don't let him hear that, she thought. He thinks badly enough of me as it is. . .

'I know you must be relieved,' said Sonia, 'so why are you looking so awful?

'I've got a splitting headache,' said Marnie.

'I knew it! Taking on all those extra patients on top of your own work. You've been overdoing again.' And Sonia rushed off to fetch Marnie some aspirin.

As if aspirin could cure my troubles, thought Marnie bitterly.

CHAPTER TEN

BY FRIDAY, it was actually being whispered that James had proposed and Marnie had turned him down. 'You've passed up a really good man there,' scolded Belle when she heard that rumour. 'Sometimes I wonder if you've not got a screw loose!'

Marnie was inclined to wonder the same thing about Belle. Divorced in her teens, widowed in her twenties, and now happily married for a third time, Belle ought to know more about men than she seemed to.

James might have kept his promise, but that didn't alter the fact that he had a very colourful reputation where women were concerned. 'You shouldn't listen to rumour, Belle,' she reproved. 'There was no proposal for me to reject. James and I parted by mutual agreement. We're incompatible,' she added firmly.

Belle answered that with a disbelieving snort and went out, banging the office door behind her.

At half-past ten, Marnie's bleep sounded for the umpteenth time that morning. She took the call in the office. 'Hi, Marnie,' breezed the irrepressible new assistant chief personnel officer. 'I'm having trouble getting a consultant for two today, so we've moved those interviews back to half-four. OK?'

Marnie just managed not to tell him she'd told him so, and asked instead if he'd managed to let all the applicants know. Three of the four were from out of town.

'Did try, Marnie, but no dice. Not to worry, we'll give 'em tea and a little tour or something.' Then he rang off, giving Marnie no chance to make any suggestions. She shrugged. Ah well, with luck they'd think it was all part of the drill.

Meeting Don Revell at four twenty-five in the boardroom, Marnie realised that he was all one with his telephone persona; he looked, she thought, more like somebody from the media than a hospital administrator. He squeezed her hands and gazed into her eyes with an expression which he obviously expected to knock her cold. 'Hello, Marnie. They told me you were gorgeous, but that's the understatement of the year! Are you doing anything tonight?'

'Yes,' she said coolly, causing him to free her hands just as the door opened and James came in.

He gave Marnie just the merest glance before transferring his gaze to Don Revell. It had him straightening his awful tie. 'Thanks for coming, Jim—Mr Dalgleish,' the ACPO amended hastily as James frowned heavily. 'Sorry we couldn't get the applications to you earlier——'

'But you were expecting Dr Leith to officiate,' James finished for him. 'Give me two minutes to glance over them, would you?' And, without waiting for assent, he sat down in the centre chair at the long polished table and opened the folder. Marnie and the personnel officer took the chairs to right and left, waiting in silence.

Marnie was acutely conscious of James so close to her. He wore a dark suit as befitted the occasion, but he must have come straight from Theatre, judging by the faint aura of anaesthetic that clung to him. She had never known him to interview physio staff before, and she wondered why he had agreed to now, with things between them the way they were.

'Right!' he said, startling Marnie out of her reverie. 'Ready when you are, Revell. Let's have the first one.'

Don Revell nodded to his secretary. 'Ask Mr Anderson to come in, would you, Lena?'

A well set up, clean-limbed boy, with a brilliant degree, splendid references; intelligent, articulate and engaging. 'I definitely want him,' said Marnie firmly, making her bid the minute the boy was out of the room.

James gave her a strange glance as though he suspected her of something more than professional partiality. Marnie coloured. Satisfied, he said, 'The boy certainly interviews well, but let's reserve judgement until we've seen the girls.'

He was going to overrule her—Marnie just knew it!

'Miss Glen,' announced the secretary. A twenty-two-year-old, newly capped and looking for her first job. Her references were kind, but hardly encouraging—of the 'means well but is rather poorly organised' variety. She was ravishingly pretty, though, and stumbled through her interview like an eager clumsy young puppy.

'And do you want her too?' James enquired silkily of Marnie when she had gone.

'Do you?' she retorted.

'I'm quite sure you think I do,' he murmured.

The third candidate was already working in Duntrune and Marnie knew nothing but good of her, but nature had not blessed her with beauty, so poor Miss Laird was as good as out of it, when two of her three interviewers were impressionable males.

Number four was something else; sultry, sexy and sinuous. 'My God, what have we got here?' muttered James under his breath as she entered the room.

One of my new assistants, for sure, thought Marnie

grimly. The girl's references were good and her CV satisfactory, so she could hardly object to her on the grounds that she would cause a riot. To her surprise, James gave the girl a hard time when it was his turn for questioning. She bore it brilliantly though, and with a confidence that seemed to impress him as much as it dismayed Marnie.

'Shall I go first?' asked Don Revell, who prided himself on his lightning decisions. 'I vote for numbers two and four. Physio is the wrong job for a man, and, as Miss Laird already has a job in the city, what's the point of rocking the boat? Besides, two and four would fairly brighten the place up, eh?' He whistled loudly.

Marnie said firmly, 'I'm going to repeat my plea for number one. That boy is quite outstanding.' She paused. 'My second choice was harder to make, but I'm going for number four. She has the right experience and I feel sure she'll be—everybody's choice.'

'Here, hear,' enthused the ACPO. 'What a cracker!'

Elbow on the table, chin in hand, James was regarding Marnie with amazement. 'Whether or not she's everybody's choice remains to be seen,' he said. 'But first I'd be very interested to hear your true reason for choosing her.'

Marnie wanted to say, because, the way she was looking at you, you'll probably overrule me, so what choice do I have?

'On paper at least, she's undoubtedly the most suitable and experienced,' she returned with wondrous restraint.

'Hm! I've heard better cases made out for choosing staff,' said James candidly, causing Marnie to flush with vexation. 'Now for my selection. Number two is a sweetie.' Surprise, surprise! 'But if she's ever to amount to anything, she'll need a good deal more guidance and help than you'd have time for, Marnie. You've not been here long enough to know this, Revell, but, even when complete, the physiotherapy establishment is woefully small for a hospital of this size.

'Now for number four. I agree with Marnie that she has the right experience, but there's something here that I don't understand. Why is a girl of her age not looking for a senior post? When I tried to get an answer to that, she dodged the issue a shade too neatly, as you'll have noticed. Also, I believe she would be a subversive influence. Therefore I think that the posts should be offered to Mr Anderson and Miss Laird. He's certainly outstanding, and Miss Laird is, to my mind, the epitome of a good physiotherapist; kind and caring, as well as obviously right on top of her job.' Having delivered himself of those totally unexpected assessments, James sat back and waited for comments.

Don Revell was playing squash in ten minutes, so he wasn't about to have a debate. 'You two know more about what's wanted than I do, so I'll leave you to battle it out,' he said, gathering up his papers. 'Just let me know by Monday morning, though—there's a dear, Marnie, and I'll get letters of appointment away with the afternoon mail. Bye, then—nice weekend, folks!'

'Yes, I'll do that,' Marnie agreed absently, still disgesting James's surprising decisions.

Once they were alone, he snapped his fingers right in her line of vision to bring her out of her trance. 'Yes?' she asked, startled.

'The choice has to be yours,' James said crisply, 'but are you quite sure you can handle that *femme fatale*?'

'I've no intention of trying,' she returned promptly. 'Of the girls, Nan Laird was my choice from the beginning.'

He gave a sigh of exasperation. 'Then why in the world did you not say so?'

'Because I didn't think she had a chance,' Marnie blurted out rashly.

'And why not?' he asked predictably.

Marnie sat a second, wondering how best to get out of the hole she'd dug for herself. 'We—ell, now. . . Don Revell didn't pick her, and I didn't think you would either. And the last candidate does have the most experience. . .'

'Would you care to tell me why you didn't think I would pick Miss Laird?'

No, Marnie most definitely would not, but as he meant to make her, she might as well get it over. 'She's not exactly pretty, is she?'

'Now we seem to be getting somewhere,' said James dangerously. 'So why not go all the way and tell me you thought I'd choose the wee one just because she's so pretty—and number four because she was offering as plain as plain to go to bed with me?'

By now Marnie was scarlet with misery and embarrassment. 'Well, really!' she blustered lamely.

'Was that intended to imply that I've misread you?' James demanded inexorably.

'Well, I. . .that is, I——'

He cut across her flounderings, rising to his feet and towering over her. 'You've just made an unwarranted and most insulting reflection on my professional judgement—to add to your long-held and equally insulting opinion of my character. I'm not sure which I resent most.' When Marnie tried to speak, he barked, 'Be quiet! It's my turn now. I've always admired your undeniably beautiful exterior, believing that you had a personality to match—if only I could reach it. But I was wrong. You're prejudiced, unfeeling, ungrateful and cold. And now I think I've wasted enough time for one day.' And with that he stalked out, leaving Marnie feeling as if she'd just been put through the shredder.

She sat on there, a shrunken miserable heap, scarcely doing more than breathe until a cleaner came in, exclaiming at the sight of her. 'Sorry, hen, but I have to do this room now. . .'

Marnie jumped up, scattering the contents of her folder. 'Yes, of course. Sorry.' She collected the papers together with trembling fingers giving the cleaner a bright, stiff smile that deceived neither of them. 'Good afternoon Mrs McAllister.' Too late, Marnie remembered that her name was Burns. Another little rumour to go the rounds. Poor Miss Firth's fairly losing the heid these days. . .

Now that she'd started thinking, Marnie couldn't stop; all the way to Physio and then all the way home. James had expressed himself rather strongly, but in essence he'd got it right. She *had* expected him to go for the two most attractive girls—and, in view of his reputation, who could blame her? Where she'd gone wrong was in letting him guess. Why had she been so stupid? True, she'd thought he'd be more likely to let her have that splendid young man if she met him halfway over Sultry Susan, but when he opted for him and Nan Laird all she had to do was say that, on reflection, she too thought Nan the better choice. Why had she not done that? Because she was so completely thrown by his decision, which didn't fit in at all with the image she'd always had of him. That was why. And, unfortunately, she'd not been able to conceal it.

But there was more. The man she'd so misjudged was also the man who had awakened in her such an explosion of desire as she had never known. He was also the man who had told her so cuttingly that she was prejudiced, unfeeling, ungrateful and cold. There was only one thing to be done now, and Marnie did it. She threw herself down on her bed and sobbed.

Some time later, Marnie was roused from her misery by the phone. Unwillingly, she stretched out for it. 'Yeth?' she lisped.

'I've been waiting for almost an hour,' said Dominic. He sounded very irritable.

Marnie had completely forgotten they had a date for a drink. She tried to ask what time it was, but she was all choked up. She found a hankie and blew her nose violently.

'Marnie?' asked Dominic doubtfully. He didn't associate such a basic human noise with one so poised and elegant.

'I've—got a very bad cold,' she apologised.

'I'm sorry to hear that, but you really should have let me know you weren't coming. As I say, I've been sitting here for nearly an hour, and a woman has just tried to pick me up.'

'P'raps you'd rather it'd been a man,' she astounded herself by muttering. In her present low state, Marnie would have preferred sympathy to a scolding.

'I didn't catch that, Marnie.'

'I was apologising,' she lied tactfully. 'I'm really sorry, but I just can't make it tonight.'

'I should think not—remember how susceptible I am to infections. Well, let me know when you've recovered.'

'I'll do that,' she agreed, listening to some indistinct conversation he seemed to be having.

'It's all right, you needn't feel too badly about letting me down,' said Dominic, sounding quite cheerful now.

'A few people from the Racquets Club have just come in, so I'm joining up with them.'

'Oh, good—I *am* glad,' said Marnie ironically.

'Will you be all right?' asked Dominic, very much as an afterthought.

'I expect so,' she returned flatly. 'Goodnight, then— dear. Have a nice evening.' Click. Marnie lay down again and stared at the ceiling. He'd be a great help if I really was sick, she thought. She hadn't expected him to come rushing round and would have been embarrassed if he had, but she couldn't help being disappointed at his lack of concern.

How different he was from James, who had laid his pride on the line to get her out of a jam. She wondered about that for a bit. Why had he done it? The only explanation she could come up with was that the charade had amused him. But did that really hold water?

Next day, Marnie put in a useful morning at her hospital desk, catching up on admin duties, shelved during the week in favour of treatments. Officially, superintendents weren't counted as clinical staff, but Marnie could never stand by and see her staff overstretched without helping out. Besides, she preferred the clinical work.

Up to date with the paperwork for the first time in weeks, she went to meet her father for lunch with a clear conscience. She would have preferred a restaurant to the University Staff Club, but her father was a creature of habit, and Saturday was Staff Club day.

It was obvious that he had something on his mind, but he didn't come out with it until they moved into the lounge for coffee. Then he said. 'I had a long talk with Rob Leith the other day.'

'Oh, yes?' Marnie responded warily.

'You've been very sly,' said her father, 'I'd no idea you were so friendly with James Dalgleish.'

Marnie adored her father, but she couldn't help thinking how much easier it would be if he was nothing to do with hospitals and never got to hear the gossip. 'I—I wouldn't have said we were friends, exactly,' she denied. 'We did go out a few times while you were away, but that's all. We're not really on the same wavelength.'

'What a pity!' His disappointment was clear. 'He's a fine young man—as well as an excellent surgeon.'

Marnie couldn't believe her ears. 'I know that men and women look at these things differently, Dad, but you must know about his reputation with women.'

'I know he's always had difficulty fighting them off,' allowed her father.

'From what *I've* heard, he hasn't always tried very hard!'

'Well, what do you expect a normal man to do? Live like a monk until he finds the one and only girl? I met your mother when I was just a third-year student and she was a very new and bewildered wee probationer. And from that day on, there was never anybody else for either of us. But not everybody is that lucky. James hasn't been—and neither have you. And that worries me. It worried your mother too. Sadly, you were the only child we were able to produce, and we hated the thought of you growing old alone—and lonely.'

'Good grief, Dad, I've only just turned twenty-eight!' breathed Marnie. 'I'd no idea you were such an old-fashioned traditionalist!'

'If that means knowing that the best chance of happiness for man or woman lies in a stable, loving marriage, then I accept the label,' said Professor Firth doggedly. 'And I'm bound to say that the men you've gone around with up to now have earned neither my confidence nor my approbation.'

This was plain speaking with a vengeance. Marnie couldn't remember ever before having such a conversation with her father. 'Are you saying that you'd be happy to see me take up with James Dalgleish?' she demanded.

'If you want the truth, I'd be delighted, but it's what you want that matters,' insisted the Professor. 'All I ask is that you give some thought to your future. There'll come a day when your work, and some poodle-faker to squire you round the entertainment circuit will no longer be enough. At least, I hope so,' he added firmly. 'I would like some grandchildren.'

Marnie was thankful that two of her father's colleagues happened by just then and stopped for a chat, because the chat soon changed to shop talk and she was able to think.

Too much was happening too fast—James's crushing assessment of her yesterday afternoon, Dominic's uncaring attitude in the evening, and now her father's astonishing outburst. She'd have thought James would be the last person her father would consider a suitable husband for her. But then Dad didn't see him as she did—though, after yesterday's eye-opener, Marnie was no longer so sure about him as she had been.

'What are you doing for the rest of the day, dear?' asked her father when his colleagues had gone.

'Eh? Oh, nothing, really.'

'Then how about coming with me to see Gran? We've not been for ages. And then after that, perhaps we could go to the theatre—if we can get seats.'

'I'd like that,' responded Marnie, brightening up as the prospect of a lonely evening receded.

'Good.' He hesitated. 'I'm sorry I sounded off like that just now, darling. How you live your life is none of my business.'

'There was a lot of truth in—everything you said,' she admitted thoughtfully. 'And, Dad—I'm so very glad you care.'

Next morning, Marnie was just out of the shower and wondering if she really wanted any breakfast when the phone rang. It was Michael Cullen, senior physiotherapist on Medical at the Royal Infirmary and duty physio this weekend. 'I'm desperately sorry, Marnie, but I've just cracked a couple of ribs,' he said as calmly as if he were reporting a cut finger.

'Michael! But how? And is that all? I mean, are you all right apart from that?'

'Yes, fine. I managed to grab the baby as she set off down the stairs and tossed her to Rosemary before I felt myself overbalancing. She was all right, but I contrived to fall from top to bottom.'

'Thank goodness you didn't break you neck!' breathed Marnie. 'Now you're not to worry. I'll take over today—and you must get along to Casualty, you hear? In fact, I'll pick you up myself on my way in.'

'There's no need——' he began, but the adrenalin was flowing freely now and Marnie overrode his protests. So, not long afterwards, Michael was being X-rayed and Marnie was sorting out the day's priorities.

Could be worse, she decided. The actual number of patients was small, as was usual for summer weekends, but several of them required treatment two hourly. So that was an empty Sunday taken care of. What's the matter with me? Marnie wondered as she made her way to the intensive care unit. I never used to think like this.

In ICU, the charge nurse greeted her with a wicked whistle. 'To what do we owe the pleasure?' he wondered.

Marnie thanked him for the lovely welcome and explained about Michael's accident, getting in return an update on the three patients she had come to treat. 'All so different, Pete, yet all needing the same treatment,' she summarised.

'Yes, it all comes down to breathing difficulties in here,' he agreed. 'Whether you arrive after a road accident like Mr Tait, from Theatre after arresting like Mrs Lennie or because you swallowed a massive dose of Valium when your boyfriend dumped you, like that poor wee lassie in the corner.'

'Love does funny things to people,' said Marnie, without thinking.

'Is that your experience, Marnie?' asked Pete curiously.

'I've never been in love,' she insisted, 'but onlookers are supposed to see most of the game—or so it's said. Can you spare me a nurse to do the suction while I percuss, or shall I just get on with it?'

'I'll come and help you myself,' he decided. 'I have to keep my hand in too, you know.'

So thanks to his help, Marnie was able to move on to Surgical sooner than she'd expected. Half a dozen patients here—most of them just for checking—and then two of Michael's chronic chests for postural drainage. Yes, she would be through the first round before lunch, despite the late start.

On the way to the canteen, Marnie made a detour via A and E to ask about Michael's fractured ribs.

'Right seven and eight snapped amidships as clean as a whistle,' said Bill Smith, the senior orthopaedic registrar, who had spent his first three doctoring years in the Royal Navy and had never forgotten it. 'But a young man like Mike should have been able to take a tumble without doing any damage, so I took a blood sample for a white cell count—just in case.'

'That was good of you, Bill,' said Marnie gratefully.

'Not really,' he denied. 'James always insists that we probe around a bit if there's anything at all atypical about the circumstances of injury.' He stopped, as though unsure how to continue. 'But then James is rather an exceptional sort of guy.'

No prizes for guessing whose side you're on! Marnie willed herself to keep smiling as she responded, 'Yes— a quite exceptional surgeon, as my father was remarking only yesterday. Thanks for looking after Michael so well—he's one of my best therapists.'

'Nobody could say you don't value your *staff*, Marnie,' said Bill as she walked away. Had she imagined that slight stressing, and, if she hadn't, what did he mean? This was her first exposure all round the hospital since her quarrel with James, so perhaps she should have been prepared for the odd innuendo. But she wasn't. Marnie began to regret stepping into the breach so readily.

By late evening, she was regretting it even more. Could be she was over-sensitive, but everybody seemed to have something to say—directly or indirectly. And except for Sister Drummond on Surgical four, who had chased James for years before giving up and marrying a patient, it was clear that the sympathy all lay with James.

And Sister Drummond was no comfort, insisting as she did on seeing Marnie as a victim. Marnie found herself making a spirited defence of James that left Sister Drummond thoroughly confused and herself rather ashamed. 'I don't care,' she muttered as she left the ward. 'Nobody talks about him like that in my hearing and gets away with it!' If she hadn't been so busy, Marnie might have wondered just why she had reacted that way, but she'd just been summoned urgently to Paediatrics.

'A sweet wee mite of sixteen weeks with bronchiolitis,' said Sister, who was waiting anxiously in the corridor.

'I didn't think this was quite the season for it,' observed Marnie, dredging up a few facts as Sister rushed her along.

'It isn't, dear, but that's what she's got right enough. The registrar hasn't seen her yet, so this call's not official. I hope you don't mind, but the wee soul is in such distress. . .'

'Of course not, Sister—I respect your judgement.' As did everybody else in the hospital.

Sister helped Marnie into a gown and stood over her like an anxious mother as, with her thumb and two fingers, Marnie skilfully vibrated the tiny chest to free the secretions that were blocking the airways. 'Would you look at that!' she breathed at the amount in the catheter after she'd applied some gentle suction.

'Yes, you'd wonder where it all came from,' agreed Sister. 'But see how her colour's improving?' She took the baby and gave her a little cuddle before strapping her carefully into the infant relax chair, which was preferred for nursing tiny babies with chest troubles. 'Thanks so much for coming so promptly, Miss Firth,' said Sister afterwards. 'Could you do with a nice cup of something now, or are you in a great hurry?'

'No, I've finished for the time being, and I'd love a cup of tea, please, Sister.'

'Then just you go and put your feet up in my office while I see about it.'

Sister was away some time, and when she returned there were three cups on the tray, along with the tea things and a plate of buttered scones. 'You're going to have some company, dear,' she explained. 'Baby Flora wasn't our only emergency admission this evening.'

Marnie waited for the others to come before pouring out, but firm footsteps in the corridor heralded one person only—James.

He stopped in the doorway, frowning. 'What the hell are you doing here?' he demanded.

Marnie scrambled to her feet, as if she could cope better standing. 'I came to treat a baby—and then Sister offered me tea.'

'Same here. Meta is very generous with the refreshments. And here she is,' he added with obvious relief.

But Sister didn't come in, just beamed at her guests and said she was sure they'd not mind looking after themselves, before shutting the door on them. Another tacit statement, perhaps?

James leaned against the wall as far from Marnie as he could get, crossed his arms and glared at her. 'Are you staying?' he barked.

Marnie didn't suppose there was anything to be gained by staying, but she wasn't going to be driven away. 'I'm as much Sister's guest as you are, so—yes! I'm staying. Are you?'

'I've no choice. I'm waiting to see some X-rays.'

'Of a child?'

'No—an elephant? What the hell did you think?'

'I think you're in a very bad temper,' said Marnie.

He scowled at her. 'So would you be if you'd seen what I've just seen—a boy of two with hardly an inch of his skin that's not bruised. He's also sustained four untreated fractures in the past six months, and now he has a broken jaw and a nasty depressed fracture at the base of the skull. If he survives, he'll be a cripple for life. What sort of monster can do that to anybody? Let alone a child!'

'Another battered baby—how dreadful!' sighed Marnie.

'"Dreadful" is an understatement. And when the case comes to court—if it ever does—some mealy-mouthed defence lawyer will stand up and say it's all society's fault. I'd like to kick his teeth in!'

'Who? The lawyer?'

'Don't be stupid—the swine who's been systematically abusing that child, of course!'

'Kicking his teeth in would only bring you down to his level,' said Marnie earnestly.

She had to sit down to bear the weight of the look James gave her then. 'Not content with teaching me a lesson on the sexual front, she's now embarking on a complete moral overhaul,' he said scathingly. 'Why do you not go into a convent and have done with it? That's certainly the best place for you!'

Marnie only really heard the first bit—the bit about teaching him a lesson. 'I don't know what you've heard, but it's not true,' she insisted.

James regarded her steadily for what felt like hours before he said, 'I've heard a lot of things in the course of what you consider to be my misspent life. Was there anything particular you had in mind?'

Marnie squared up to him, her eyes bright with determination. 'I never set out to teach you a lesson—not in private, and not in public. I've been telling everybody who'll listen that we parted by mutual agreement because we discovered we'd really nothing in common. And I'll go on saying that. I'll even write an open letter and put it on the noticeboard in the canteen if you like! Because that's how grateful I am

to you for saving my face.' Marnie needed a deep
breath before she could continue. 'And I'm sorry I said
what I did about you and the fiend who attacked that
child. I'd like to kick his teeth in too. And now I think
I'll leave,' she wound up hastily, her courage being
almost all used up.

James didn't try to stop her. Was he too astonished,
or was it that he simply didn't care?

Oh, well said, Marnie. Very well said indeed, she
told herself. There was only one thing wrong with all
those brave words back there. You *did* tell Fiona you
were out to teach James a lesson; something she'd
obviously passed on to the other physios, who had
repeated it all round the hospital.

The thing was that when Marnie spoke to Fiona she
was trying to save her own pride. Now her main interest
was in saving his.

CHAPTER ELEVEN

AUGUST had given way to September, and now there was often a nip in the air, morning and evening. Michael was back on the job long since, the two new physios had taken up their posts and Fiona had won her battle to remain at the Royal. Things in the department were as good as they were ever likely to be, and, because everybody thought she should, Marnie had taken a holiday. She had gone to Edinburgh, just catching the tail-end of the Festival, and spending far too much money on clothes.

Sonia had wanted to know why not Italy or Bermuda or some other such exotic place, and Marnie had said it wasn't much fun going abroad on one's own. Sonia then asked why she didn't go with Dominic, to which Marnie replied that she wouldn't want to give him ideas. Marnie couldn't care less about Dominic's ideas; it was James she didn't want picking up wrong signals. Though why she was bothered she couldn't imagine. James couldn't have made it more plain that he didn't care a damn about her. On the odd occasions when their paths crossed these days, he was back to treating her the way he always had; with that mixture of humour and good nature with which he treated everybody. That fatal mixture that had misled so many impressionable girls in the past, and would no doubt mislead a good few more before he was done.

Marnie would have preferred him to keep up his former critical reserve. Then she could have gone on

thinking he felt *something* different for her alone—
even if it was only disapproval.

She opened her wardrobe that evening and eyed its
contents with no enthusiasm. Dominic hadn't said
where they were going tonight, so she presumed they'd
be eating at the Blue Crocodile, along with all the
other dressed-up, well-heeled yuppies. She'd better not
let him down. Grab one of the new Edinburgh outfits,
then, all so far unworn.

Dominic was already there when Marnie arrived. In
his pale grey suit and Italian silk shirt, he looked
exactly what he was; a man going onwards and upwards
in the cut-and-thrust world of high finance. His hazel
eyes gleamed appreciatively behind a new pair of horn-
rimmed specs as he watched Marnie's entrance—so
neat and so well groomed in cream and yellow from
head to toe. 'Nobody would ever suspect you worked
in a hospital,' he told her, having planted a chaste kiss
on each of her smooth cheeks.

Marnie eyed him sideways. 'Was that a compliment?'

'But of course. None of the few colleagues of yours
I've met was outstanding for sartorial elegance.'

'I expect that has something to do with income,'
Marnie retorted flatly. 'We don't go in for productivity
bonuses and company cars in the NHS.'

'You've obviously had a hard day, dear,' Dominic
said soothingly. 'Never mind—the wine's just coming,'
he added, like somebody suggesting it's time I took my
Valium, thought Marnie.

Not Valium, but Vouvray, a good vintage and properly chilled, but Marnie was hungry. She reached for
the crisps and a couple of olives.

Dominic frowned. 'Darling, you'll cloud the bouquet,' he said, trying so hard to be patient. He only
ever called her darling when he was really upset.

Marnie withdrew her hand. 'That would be—a pity,' she said. 'Only I didn't each much lunch today.' Now that the pressure was off, she sometimes went to the staff canteen, but seeing James lunching there with his new housewoman had put her right off her food.

'I only had a snack myself today, while awaiting a call from Hong Kong,' said Dominic. And I'm not making a pig of *myself*, Marnie finished for him in her mind. She knew Dominic's snacks—smoked salmon and a half-bottle of hock, most likely.

'Are we eating here?' she asked.

'We can if you'd rather, but I've booked a table at that new place down by the docks that everybody's talking about.'

Marnie had heard of Tradewinds too—at the hospital. The general opinion was that it was excellent, but pricey. Had Dominic had a rise, then?' 'That sounds like fun, dear,' she said. 'No, no more wine for me, thanks.' Not on an empty stomach and when I'm wearing four-inch heels. I might trip and measure my length, and then what price your standing with all these yuppies?

Coming out of the wine-bar, Dominic cracked one of his little jokes. 'Your car or mine, dear?' he asked, having already taken out his keys.

'It's rather uncivilised down by the docks,' warned Marnie. 'I really do think we should take mine—it'd attract less attention.'

'On the other hand, we might be *seen*,' said Dominic. They certainly would be—by somebody—but Marnie knew what he meant. Rising young financiers simply did not go about in Ford Fiestas. She gave her little car a comforting pat as she passed it by, and got into the Merc.

The new restaurant was every bit as good as its

reputation. Marnie loved the crab bisque, was enjoying her salmon *en croute* and was really looking forward to strawberries Romanoff, when something happened that not only took away her appetite, but actually made her feel sick. Looking round the room, she spotted James at a table in the corner, with his very good friend Helen Ballantyne, doyenne of Theatre. But wait—was there not somebody else with them? Another quick peep gave her a glimpse of Bill Smith, the senior registrar. Satisfied, she sat back and slightly to the left so that the table-lamp would hide her from view. It wasn't long, though, before she felt the need for another look in order to see how far on they were with their meal. Was there a chance they'd finish and leave before she did? Take as long as you can over this, Marnie.

When the waiter kept them waiting rather long for their dessert, Dominic got restless. Marnie smoothed him down, or tried to, but he snapped his fingers at the waiter and made a fuss. James would never have done that—but then James was never kept waiting.

'Coffee, dear?' asked Dominic when Marnie had made her strawberries last as long as she could.

'Yes, please, dear. It will round off this delicious meal perfectly.' I shall ask for a second cup and a third, if necessary. . .

That was when James gave out with one of his great musical guffaws. His companions were laughing too. Some sort of celebration was in progress; at any rate, there was much clinking of glasses going on in their corner.

Dominic turned round and glared. 'This place will not enhance its reputation if it encourages people of that sort,' he said when he turned back.

Marnie felt an enormous surge of anger which she

didn't try to control. 'The man who laughed is a dedicated and much respected surgeon,' she hissed. 'And to my certain knowledge, the three of them have spent at least six hours in a hot and stuffy theatre today, performing some very difficult and important operations. They've earned some relaxation!'

Dominic said nothing—he was too surprised. Marnie, beautiful, *soignée* Marnie, who was always so cool, poised and wellbred, was behaving like a lioness defending her cubs. She was flushed and her lovely violet eyes flashed fire. He hardly recognised her.

When he did react, it was entirely in character. 'Please keep your voice down, darling. There may be people here who know me.'

'So what? There are at least three people here who definitely know me! And please don't call me darling again—unless you mean it!'

Dominic summoned up all his dignity. 'I don't think we'll wait for coffee,' he said awfully. 'Waiter—the bill!'

Marnie put some notes on the table—this certainly was turning out to be a night for going Dutch!—and then she began inching round the edge of the room, praying she could get out without being spotted.

She didn't quite make it. 'Marnie—hey, Marnie!' called Helen. 'Come right over here this minute and congratulate us!'

Reluctantly Marnie turned round and went towards them, smiling stiffly. 'Somebody's won the Pools,' she suggested.

'Better than that,' said Helen. 'We're engaged. He's popped the question at last!'

Marnie went rigid and stopped breathing.

'Yes, right between a pin and plate and an ampu-

tation,' supplemented James, who was watching
Marnie carefully. 'How's that for timing?'

She forced herself to look at him without wavering.
'Just about perfect, I'd say.' Then she leaned down to
kiss Helen. 'I hope you'll be very happy,' she managed.
Then she held out her hand to James.

He took it and passed it across the table to Bill.
'You've got the wrong man,' he said tonelessly.
'Helen's far too sensible to listen to any blandishments
of mine.'

Marnie felt herself relaxing. 'You lucky old thing,'
she said gaily, kissing Bill too. Helen had said 'at last',
but this was one hospital romance of which she hadn't
had an inkling. 'So when's it to be?'

'Not before the next pay rise,' said Bill with an
engaging grin. 'Are you on your own, then, Marnie?
Because why not——' He stopped abruptly when
Helen kicked him under the table.

He hadn't seen Dominic waiting impatiently by the
door, but Helen had. 'I think Marnie is with someone,
dear,' she said warningly.

She looks upset, thought Marnie. I wonder why?
Probably Bill doesn't know about her and James being
so friendly, and I went and let the cat out of the bag,
me and my big mouth. It didn't occur to her that
Helen, who had thought Marnie was alone, might be
trying to spare her old friend James some pain and
embarrassment.

James was also looking past Marnie with an
expression of scorn. She turned and saw Dominic. 'I'd
better be going,' she mumbled.

'Thank you for not introducing me,' said Dominic
stiffly as he pushed through the swing door in front of
her.

'I knew you'd rather I didn't,' she was saying just as

stiffly when Dominic stopped dead on the pavement, ashen-pale and trembling. Marnie stared at him in astonishment, then followed the direction of his outstretched hand.

The beautiful white Mercedes parked at the kerbside was white no longer, but as dazzlingly colourful as a disco. It was also leaning drunkenly to one side, having lost two of its wheels. 'Oh, how awful!' she breathed.

'Awful?' he squeaked, hopping with rage and almost in tears. 'It's catastrophic! I could get the sack for this!'

'What nonsense,' said Marnie bracingly. 'Come along—we'll go to the police station. Somebody might have seen something. There's a gang of young vandals around here, and this looks like their work.'

'Oh, my beautiful car! What shall I do?'

Pull yourself together and stop behaving like a hysterical schoolgirl for a start, thought Marnie. Any minute now those three will come out, and if James sees you in this state my stock will go down even lower.

Yes, even now she could hear people coming out. 'Come on, for God's sake *move*, Dominic! No, not that way, you shouldn't touch the car——'

'Quite right,' said James, taking in the situation at once and walking all round Dominic's wounded beauty. 'There doesn't seem to be any major damage, but I suppose this means you're stranded.' He fingered his formidable jaw. 'Look here, you'll be wanting to call in at the police station, but afterwards come to the hospital. I'll be going into town soon, so I can give you a lift.'

'We—we could get a taxi,' stammered Marnie, torn two ways.

'But if this man is going into town anyway, Marnie,' said Dominic. James's brisk manner seemed to have brought him out of shock. 'My name is Keith, by the way. Dominic Keith, Mr er—er——'

'James Dalgleish. See you in about twenty minutes, then.' And without another glance for Marnie, James bounded after Helen and Bill, strolling on ahead, hand in hand.

'The forceful type,' said Dominic then with something of a sneer.

'Wimps don't make good surgeons. They don't have the bottle for it!' snapped Marnie, furious on James's behalf. How generous he is, and how capable—compared with you! she thought.

'That's the second time you've leapt to his defence,' complained Dominic. 'You're very loyal. How well do you know that man?'

'Well enough to respect and admire him very much! As do most people, including my father. Here's the police station.'

'Are you sure? It looks more like an Army post.'

'And very suitable too—in a district like this,' said Marnie.

The desk sergeant dealt very efficiently with them. He was sympathetic too—up to a point. 'If I may say so, sir, it wasn't just the wisest thing to leave a valuable car like yours unattended in a district like this.'

More or less what Marnie had said when suggesting they took her car, but that didn't save her from Dominic's wrath. 'You should have told me this could happen,' he said waspishly as soon as they got outside.

'I tried to, but you wouldn't listen. You were too worried about your image!'

'I don't like your tone!' he snapped.

'And I like yours even less!' By the time they reached the hospital, they were quarrelling violently, and if James had not been waiting at the gate in his car with the engine running Marnie would have parted company with Dominic there and then. 'Don't you dare let me down,' she snarled at him, before smiling uncertainly at James and saying, 'Just so long as this isn't too much trouble. . .'

'If it were, I'd not have offered,' he said. 'Surely you know me well enough to realise that? Where to?'

'Bank Street would be fine—if it's not out of your way.'

'Bang on course. Get in, then.'

After a second's pause, Marnie got in the back beside Dominic, but sitting as far away from him as possible.

It took fifteen minutes to town from the Royal, and as nobody spoke it was an uncomfortable journey. They were nearly there when they saw ahead what appeared to be a multiple crash at a busy crossroads.

"Quick! Turn left here and you can avoid that,' quavered Dominic turning pale again.

But James was in the business of coping with accidents, not avoiding them. He put on speed to reach the scene more quickly, parked on the pavement and sprinted the rest of the way. Spurred by the same instincts, Marnie got out and ran after him.

The damaged cars were slewed at crazy angles across the road and a motorcycle was lying on its side, one wheel still spinning. Beside it, a man lay on his back in the road, with blood spurting in great fountains from an ugly gash in his thigh.

James dropped on his knees and, making a ramrod of his right arm, he thrust his clenched fist hard into the man's abdomen, compressing the abdominal aorta. 'For God's sake somebody dial 999!' he shouted.

Marnie sent a bystander into the nearest pub to phone, and, having checked that none of the occupants of the cars was seriously hurt, she demanded a large spanner from one bemused driver and hurried back to James, dragging off her scarf as she went. With hands that trembled, she got it under the patient's thigh above the gash, and tied it firmly. The she slipped in the spanner, turning and turning. . .

James glanced sideways. 'That's my brave girl—tight as you can, now.' He had already slowed the flow of blood, but it would start up again if he released his pressure on the main artery before the tourniquet was tight enough. When he judged the time was right, James removed his fist and took over from Marnie.

By the time two ambulances arrived, the loss of blood had slowed to a trickle. 'Somebody knows his first aid,' commented one attendant. 'Come on, then, Denis, take over from the gentleman. Well done, squire! You been in the Army?'

'The Marines,' lied James, getting thankfully off his knees and pulling Marnie up too. They were both liberally splashed with blood and their clothes were ruined. Satisfied that the ambulance crews could cope, James drew Marnie away. 'This is where we fade out of the picture before one of them recognises us under all this gore,' he murmured as a police panda car screeched to a halt beside them, lights flashing.

Not surprisingly, they were taken for casualties until James explained. 'And before you ask, Constable, we didn't see what happened. The crash occurred before we arrived.'

'But we'll need names and addresses, though, sir.'

'Of course.' Marnie hardly needed to say a thing. She just stood there, lost in admiration at the way James was handling this. It took time, though, and it was quite dark before they were free to go.

They were in the car again and had gone several yards before Marnie remembered Dominic. She peered over her shoulder into the back. 'He's gone!' she exclaimed.

'I was wondering when you'd remember him,' James said impassively.

'Well, that was enough to make anybody forget anything.' She peered out of the window. 'I wonder where he's gone?'

'Into the nearest pub,' James suggested contemptuously. 'The puir wee mannie has had a nasty shock.'

'He's—very sensitive and easily upset,' Marnie defended.

'No wonder you stick with him, then.'

'I *beg* your pardon?'

'The man's a wimp,' said James. 'But since you don't like real men, he's just the sort for you. Easily handled and—undemanding!' His meaning was crystal-clear.

'That's not fair,' she whispered. She meant his assessment of her, but James thought she was still defending Dominic.

He stopped the car. 'I give up,' he said wearily. 'Get out, then.'

'Why?' she asked.

'Well, you want to go and look for your beloved, do you not?'

'He'll be all right. Why wouldn't he be?'

'A moment ago, you seemed to think he might be having a nervous breakdown.'

'You do exaggerate,' she said. 'Anyway, I couldn't possibly—not in this state. Look at me! And you. . . Good God, we look as if we'd just murdered somebody! Besides, he isn't.'

'Isn't what?'

'My beloved. And what's more, you know he isn't. I told you that we're just good friends. Or were,' she corrected, because she knew quite definitely that

Dominic would never want to see her again after tonight.

James made no comment; just restarted the car and drove on. A minute later he said in a markedly gentler tone, 'You did very well back there. For a girl who can't stand Theatre.'

'That was different—it was an emergency. That poor man was bleeding to death.'

'I guess you are your father's daughter after all,' he said as they turned in at the gateway to her flats.

'You've brought me home!' she exclaimed. She'd suddenly remembered her car, parked in Bank Street, but she wasn't going to mention that.

'It would have been much nearer to go to my place to clean up, but I thought you might misunderstand. Besides, we were able to get here via some little-used back streets. . .'

'Whereas you can only get to your house by driving along the prom, which is brilliantly lit.'

'That's very true.'

'And with the police patrolling there so frequently, trying to catch folk speeding—and as you've got even more blood on you than I have. . .'

'I would have some explaining to do if I was seen,' agreed James.

'So perhaps you'd care to come in for a wash,' suggested Marnie, heart thumping. If he refuses, she thought, then I shall know there's no hope——

'I'd really appreciate that,' said James.

'I think we should take the lift,' said Marnie when they had crept unseen into the building.

'Good thinking,' said James. And then, 'One would almost think you were used to coming home in this state,' he added as they soared upwards.

'Not since I was ten and fell off a wall on to a hay

rake.' Marnie opened the lift door and peeped out. 'All clear—quick, though.' She bolted down the hall to get her key in the lock.

When they were inside her flat with the door safely shut, Marnie tried not to remember all his other visits. She opened a door. 'Here's the bathroom—I think you'll find everything you need.' Then she turned tail and fled. James had already removed his jacket and was unbuttoning his shirt, and she wasn't sure she could bear the sight of his naked torso without throwing herself at him, in her present emotional state.

While her father was abroad, Marnie had gone through his wardrobe, cleaning and mending, and not everything had been returned. She found a pair of light golf trousers and a blue striped shirt. She shook her head doubtfully. Probably not large enough, but a boon in the circumstances. James's own clothes were soaked and completely unwearable.

She left them outside the bathroom. 'I've put some clean clothes outside the door for you,' she called, retreating again.

It was ridiculous to feel so nervous. Given the same circumstances, she'd do this for anybody. Only James wasn't anybody. He was the man she loved and desired above any man on earth. And something was telling her that this was a chance—perhaps her last chance— to patch things up between them. If only she could get it right.

In the en-suite off her bedroom, Marnie stripped off and showered quickly. Afterwards, she toyed with the idea of putting on a sexy silk dressing-gown, decided that was too obvious and slipped into jeans and a loose blouson top instead.

She found James prowling round the living-room, scowling. His borrowed trousers were just about adequate, but he hadn't been able to button the shirt. 'I only put these on because my own things are ruined,' he said savagely.

Marnie blinked. 'I know that—and I'm sorry they're a bit on the small side, but I don't keep a selection, you know.'

'I should hope not! Surely one at a time is enough!'

'One what?' she queried.

'I could think of several things to call him, but Dominic is not one!'

'Oh, I get it!' snapped Marnie. 'On the way here, you accused me of being some sort of nutter who doesn't like men. Now you're assuming I keep one in the house. Make up your mind—you can't have it both ways!'

'Any man would have made the same assumption,' growled James.

'Not if he was a gentleman, he wouldn't! Those things you're wearing belong to my father. And if you don't believe me, you can ring him up and ask him. Go on—there's the phone. There!' She pointed to it as though he'd never recognise it for himself. 'And if you *dare* to say he'll only say yes to cover for me——'

'You've got a nasty suspicious mind!'

'*I've* got a nasty suspicious mind? I like that!'

They glared at one another, breathless and heaving, furious and miserable.

'Oh, Marnie. . .' he groaned.

'James. . .' Tentatively she held out her hands.

They came together in relief and desperation. Kissing, murmuring regrets and pleas for forgiveness, then kissing again.

'Oh, my darling! I thought I'd lost you, my little love.'

'So did I—— Oh, James! Can you ever forgive me?'

'Darling, it was all my fault for going about it in that daft way. Only I couldn't think how to reach you.'

'What do you mean?' asked Marnie, bewildered.

'For years you resisted every attempt I made to get near you. So when the opportunity presented, I took it. It wasn't the way I'd have chosen to court you, but frankly, my love, I was getting desperate. And then when you burst out at me that night. . .'

'Oh, darling, don't remind me!'

'But why did you? Everything seemed to be so right between us by then.'

'I thought—oh, I don't know what I thought! Yes, I do—I was afraid. And jealous. People kept telling me about some girl in Glasgow.'

'Dorothy,' he said. 'I think we were both weary of the relationship by then. I hadn't seen her for weeks, and we ended it the day after you and I quarrelled. She seemed as relieved as I was. But then we'd always said that if one of us fell in love. . .' His eyes blazed into hers. 'Oh, Marnie—I love you so much!'

'And I absolutely adore you, James,' she whispered.

'So does that mean that you——?'

'Of course it does, my darling.'

'But first I think I will make that phone call.'

'You don't believe me about the clothes!' she wailed.

'Hush, my love—of course I do. But before I take them off, I'd like to ask the owner if it's all right for me to marry his daughter.'

Marnie knew what the answer would be, but she couldn't resist asking, 'What will you do if he says it isn't?'

'I shall pretend I've suddenly gone deaf,' said James very firmly.

Love is in the Air...

Mills & Boon have commissioned four of your favourite authors to write four tender romances.

Guaranteed love and excitement for St. Valentine's Da

A BRILLIANT DISGUISE	-	Rosalie Ash
FLOATING ON AIR	-	Angela Devine
THE PROPOSAL	-	Betty Neels
VIOLETS ARE BLUE	-	Jennifer Taylor

Available from January 1993   PRICE £3.99

4 MEDICAL ROMANCES
AND 2 FREE GIFTS
From Mills & Boon

Capture all the excitement, intrigue and emotion of the busy medical world by accepting four FREE Medical Romances, plus a FREE cuddly teddy and special mystery gift. Then if you choose, go on to enjoy 4 more exciting Medical Romances every month! Send the coupon below at once to:

**MILLS & BOON READER SERVICE, FREEPOST
PO BOX 236, CROYDON, SURREY CR9 9EL.**
No stamp required

---- ✂ --------------------------------- ✂ ----

YES! Please rush me my 4 Free Medical Romances and 2 Free Gifts! Please also reserve me a Reader Service Subscription. If I decide to subscribe, I can look forward to receiving 4 Medical Romances every month for just £6.40, delivered direct to my door. Post and packing is free, and there's a free Mills & Boon Newsletter. If I choose not to subscribe I shall write to you within 10 days - I can keep the books and gifts whatever I decide. I can cancel or suspend my subscription at any time. I am over 18.

EP19D

Name (Mr/Mrs/Ms) _____

Address _____

_____

_____ Postcode _____

Signature _____

— MEDICAL ❤ ROMANCE —

The books for enjoyment this month are:

PLAYING THE JOKER Caroline Anderson
ROMANCE IN BALI Margaret Barker
SURGEON'S STRATEGY Drusilla Douglas
HEART IN JEOPARDY Patricia Robertson

❤   ❤   ❤   ❤   ❤

Treats in store!

Watch next month for the following absorbing stories:

RAW DEAL Caroline Anderson
A PRIVATE ARRANGEMENT Lilian Darcy
SISTER PENNY'S SECRET Clare Mackay
SURGEON FROM FRANCE Elizabeth Petty